# COURT OF MEMORIES

*Forbidden Queen Book Two*

## DYAN CHICK

Illaria Publishing

Published by Illaria Publishing LLC

Cover Artwork by Sanja Balan (Sanja's Covers)
Editing by Elizabeth A. Lance (EAL Editing Services)

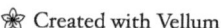 Created with Vellum

# Chapter One

ormac had insisted that we ride to Queen's Palace at the heart of Faerie. When I asked why we didn't just slide there, I was given excuses about protocol and manners. All of his excuses circled my mind as I lay awake, sleep refusing to come. It was hard enough to ease my mind in the strange room in Tristan's Palace in the Winter Court. I wasn't exactly feeling tired yet, and I wasn't sure I could sleep anyway with the excitement and fear of traveling to see the Queen.

I knew I should rest, as another several day journey was ahead of me. But sleep wouldn't come. Tristan and the other princes didn't seem to get along, yet they were willing to combine forces to help me. I wondered what the Queen was going to think when I arrived at her palace with a prince from each of the three Faerie Courts and prince from the Winter Court. I wanted to know more about the politics in this land because I felt like I was going in blind. I wondered if entering the Queen's Court with Tristan would be seen as an insult.

I turned onto my side, trying to will away all the unanswered questions. The purpose of going to see the Queen was to ask for help so I could understand at least how to channel the magic I had so I didn't keep attracting creatures from the Under. Cormac spoke of the Queen with such high regard, that I found I wasn't exactly worried about meeting her. I hoped she'd be able to help me. Secretly, I hoped she would have some insight as to where it came from. So far, all I gathered was that the magic I had shouldn't exist.

My bedroom door opened a crack and I sat up. "Who's there?"

"I didn't mean to wake you," Tristan said. "I was just making my nightly rounds."

I narrowed my eyes at the beautiful prince standing in my doorway. I had a feeling he wasn't checking on all of his guests the way he was checking on me. "Is this your normal night time routine?"

"It is when I have a beautiful female staying at my palace," he said.

"And here I thought I was special." I couldn't help but give him a little bit of attitude. Tristan certainly didn't shy away from being the center of attention. He had to be one of the most confident beings I'd ever met.

"I entertain my share of ladies." Tristan winked.

"Is that supposed to impress me?" I asked.

He shrugged. "I'm not sure yet. So far, I've gathered that you turned down the Summer Fae in favor of the Spring Prince. Which means you either don't know the reputation he carries or you don't care about sex. There's something else you're after. You're difficult to read and that's not typical for me."

Suddenly, I remembered Angela's comments about the Winter Fae in their ability to see the future. I'd experienced a couple of small moments where it was possible I was seeing things that hadn't yet happened, but it was difficult to be sure. If it was truly a gift of sight or if it was my imagination getting the better of me. "Do you normally read people? Angela said Winter Fae can see the future. Can you see mine?"

"Don't you know it's rude to ask a Winter Fae that question?" He lifted an eyebrow as he smirked.

I swallowed against a lump that had risen in my throat. His words were smooth and seemed to caress every inch of my skin. He was dangerous, yes. Like a wolf acting tame. Only I knew, if I went to feed him, it was possible he would bite off my hand.

"Sweet dreams, Cassia," Tristan said. Then he closed the door and I heard his footsteps fade away.

಄಄಄

I TURNED OVER AGAIN, away from the door, hoping that was the last of the intruders for the evening. I wondered if I should have taken Ethan or Dane up on their offers to sleep in my room with me. I had a feeling Tristan's comments about me not getting any rest with either of them in my room were accurate. It was strange to think about the fact that I had lost my virginity to someone that wasn't my husband, to someone that wasn't even human.

For a moment I wondered what Nani would think and then I realized Nani was Fae, herself. My heart ached at the thought of her and I hoped wherever she was, she had escaped my father's wrath. After seeing how powerful Fae magic was, I had to hope that Nani had magic of her own that she had called on to get away from my father.

I thought back to my time with Ethan. Everything about it felt right and natural. Even when I had been with Dane, I couldn't even find a single flicker of regret. Warmth spread through me and I smiled. I guess, I did feel a little different. I felt a little more confident.

Letting go of the human morals and following my own intuition hadn't resulted in anything catastrophic. I enjoyed myself, and I wanted to do it again. Perhaps I was going to make it in this world. Maybe having magic from all three Courts was a fluke and the Queen could help me tame it. Maybe by the end of this week,

I'd be settling into my new routine in this world, whatever that may be.

As long as I could find a way to keep these princes in my life, I would be happy here. I couldn't imagine being anywhere without them. Even Cormac, as serious as he was, felt like he was part of me now and I wouldn't trade my time with them for anything.

I snuggled under the blankets, feeling more calm and more at peace than I had in years. I knew tomorrow was going to bring changes, traveling with Tristan was going to bring its own set of challenges. But I was ready for the next phase, ready to embrace my new life as a Fae, and ready to leave the fears and frailty of being a human behind.

❦

"CASSIA, IT'S DAYBREAK," Ethan said gently.

Groggily, I opened my eyes and blinked up at Ethan's handsome face. I greeted him with a sleepy smile and reached my fingers toward his cheek, brushing them against his skin. As confident as I had been before I went to bed last night, I still wanted to make sure this was all real. I wanted to make sure that Ethan was still here, and that he was still mine. "Good morning."

Ethan leaned down and kissed my forehead. "Breakfast is ready and soon it will be time to go."

"She going to come? Or am I going to have to carry her down?"

I turned toward the newcomer and couldn't help but smile at Dane's huge grin. "She's coming," I said, throwing the covers off of me. Though, part of me wasn't completely opposed to the idea of Dane throwing me over his shoulder. A vision flashed through my mind and I saw the world from upside down as Dane walked with me over his shoulder. It faded nearly as quickly as it had arrived, leaving me with a smile. "Can you imagine the look on Cormac's face if you came down to breakfast carrying me?"

"It would be pure jealousy," Dane said. "And worth every second." He charged me, ducking down to scoop me up and throw me over his shoulder, just as I had visualized.

I squealed and giggled as Dane raced out of the room causing me to bob up and down on his muscled shoulder. "Dane, put me down, you beast!"

"Not until I see that look on Cormac's face," Dane said.

From my vantage point, I had a very clear view of Dane's firm buttocks and I felt my cheeks heat at the memory of him without his clothes on. I looked up to see Ethan trailing behind us, laughing.

"I'm not healing you if Cormac decides to punch that grin off your face," Ethan said.

"It'll still be worth it," Dane said.

I'd given up asking for him to put me down, I was laughing too hard to speak anymore anyway. The mood was lighter this morning now that the Sodalis were gone and everyone had a full night's sleep. No one seemed all that bothered by the fact that we had to go see the Queen. And I wondered how much of that was for my benefit and how much of it was because of their station.

I tried not to think about how my father had reacted every time someone with higher rank than him came by our house. He was a ball of stress, preparing and working round-the-clock to placate and impress other human beings who had nothing on him other than a title. Yet, when those people were around each other, there was no sense of fear or anxiety. My males were all royalty themselves. And though I didn't understand the way the Fae Court worked, I still knew they were high-ranking enough that going to see the Queen wasn't the same as someone like me going to see her.

Dane took the stairs carefully down to Tristan's grand dining hall. I couldn't see what was in front of us, so I watched Ethan's face to get a sense of how Cormac was going to react to the three of us acting like children.

Ethan pressed his lips together, trying to maintain some sense of decorum so I knew Cormac was in the room.

"I brought you something," Dane said.

I could only assume he was speaking to Cormac. Then, Dane burst out laughing and Ethan joined him.

"Just put her down," Cormac said.

"Now I understand how Faerie lost the Winter Court," Tristan said. "The second you think you've defeated your foes, you begin to celebrate."

"Not all of us," Cormac said. "And we granted the Winter Court its succession; the Winter Court didn't earn it."

The mood in the room shifted. It felt like every speck of happiness had been sucked out.

Dane set me down on the ground. "You know, the Winter Court could learn a lot from us. When you're kind to females and make them laugh, you don't have to force them to come to you."

Tristan lifted an eyebrow. "You want to go down memory lane?"

"That's enough," Ethan said. "We've all agreed to help Cassia reach the Queen. Our personal histories can't be brought into this. Past is past."

Tristan leaned back in his chair and stared at Cormac. I glanced over at the Autumn Prince and could almost see the fire in his gaze. His hatred for Tristan wasn't just based on his alliance to Faerie, that was clear. I didn't know what was going on between the two of them, but I knew that the sooner we reached the Queen, the better. That was, if we could get there before the two of them tried to kill each other.

Breakfast was a silent affair, which made the careful footsteps of the servants in blue sound thunderous. Wordlessly, they set plates in front of us and refilled drinks as the Fae males ate more than I thought possible for anyone to consume in one meal. Finally, I couldn't take the silence anymore.

"Why can't we just slide to the Queen's palace?" I asked.

"There are protocols," Cormac said.

"But it can be done," Tristan said. "My guess is that Cormac is testing me, dear. It has nothing to do with you."

Cormac's jaw tightened, but he didn't respond to the comment.

I wondered how we were going to survive any amount of time with the two of them together.

# Chapter Two

❧❦❧

Tristan insisted on providing horses from his stables for each of us. I felt bad that Starlight, the horse that had taken me through my time in this land so far, was still waiting for me at the stables in Twin Falls. "We told them we'd be back soon," I said to Cormac. I knew he would understand how I felt and to what I was referring.

"The horses are well cared for, my friend and I have an agreement," he said.

"How was it that you came to befriend the owner of the Dizzy Dragon?" I asked.

"I spent some time in my younger years in the Orc kingdom. I got to know many of those who live there," Cormac said.

"So he's an orc." I thought it rude to ask, but now that I knew, it made sense. I'd always assumed Orcs were wild and lacked manners. In every story I'd ever heard, they were the villain.

"Don't let his exterior fool you, that Orc is just a big softy," Cormac said.

"Oh, to be fair, he is a rare example of his kind," Dane said. "Not a good idea to just assume everyone will be your friend."

"Orc or Fae," Ethan added.

"That's true," Cormac mumbled.

"So, basically it's no different than the human world. Don't trust someone unless you get to know them and assume everyone always want something from you," I said.

"Maybe you *are* Winter Fae," Tristan said.

"We don't know what she is yet," Ethan said. "And if we want to get there in a decent amount of time we should probably get going."

"And here I thought Cormac was still boss," Tristan said.

"Unlike the Winter Court, we in Faerie believe in equality," Cormac said.

"Only for those who are highborn with magic in their veins," Tristan said. "Or have you since granted citizenship to your serving class?"

I turned from Tristan to Cormac, my brow furrowed. "What does that mean?"

"There are some things about the way our kingdom is run that have been going on for a long time," he said.

"That doesn't make those things right," Tristan said.

"You two can argue about politics later," Dane said. "Ethan's right, we don't leave now, we'll only get a few hours in before sunset. Might even add an extra day to this trip. And none of us want that."

"If this is going to be too much trouble," I said, "one of you could take me to the Queen. It doesn't have to be all of you." My heart ached at the words, I didn't want to leave any of them behind, well maybe Tristan. But I didn't want the fighting to continue.

"I'd be happy to take you, but something tells me none of these three would allow it," Tristan said.

"That's the truth," Dane said.

"Cassia, once we find out which Court you belong to, you become the responsibility of that prince as a citizen of that court, since we don't know..." Ethan trailed off.

"Do you take this much care for all of your citizens?" I asked.

"Probably not, no," Ethan said. "But it isn't typical to meet a changeling who has the power of three courts."

At least he was honest, but it still didn't make anything easier. "Then we should get going."

I watched the stable boy as he readied our horses. All four of them were large creatures, white like the snow, with gray leather saddles, and gray saddlebags. In the clothing we wore, all of us would look the part of Tristan's court. I wondered if that was on purpose to prevent anyone who might see us from knowing who we all really were or if all the clothes in Tristan's palace were this color. It felt odd to be uniformed in such a way. Though, I still wasn't sure who I was, I certainly didn't feel like I was a Winter Fae. I didn't like games or deception and I had a feeling Tristan lived for those.

"Can you ride?" Tristan asked as he lightly touched my elbow.

I turned to him. "I can ride just fine."

"She's an excellent rider," Cormac said.

Compliments from the Autumn prince were rare and I felt my cheeks flush at his words.

Someone handed me the reins to one of the large white horses and a stable boy slid a stool in front of me. Without waiting for instruction, I climbed into the saddle. "I thought we were leaving."

Cormac grinned at me before mounting his own horse.

"This way," Tristan called, leading the way.

I expected the Winter Court to be dusted with snow and I expected that the thick dress and fur-lined boots would still leave me feeling the chill in the air. But for some reason, it wasn't any cooler than it had been in the Autumn Court. My breath came out in clouds so I knew the air was colder, but I wasn't feeling the sting of the winter air on my cheeks. I wore thin, flexible riding gloves that allowed me to have complete range of motion with my fingers. Everything Tristan had provided for me to wear was nicer than anything I usually wore. Part of me felt guilty for how much he and the others had provided for me. I knew I wouldn't be able to repay their kindness.

I let my mind wander to the landscape, trying to eliminate the sinking feeling creeping in on me. In the human realm, I knew there'd be a price for all of this. Based on the Fae lore I'd heard, I knew they often dealt in favors. Yet, the only verbal agreement that had passed between me and any of the princes was one with Tristan regarding my knowledge of humans. And he hadn't brought it up once since initially asking. I wondered if he forgot. It seemed a silly favor in the first place, but he had made it seem important. Perhaps in light of the Sodalis attacks and the risk I posed to Faerie, it no longer mattered to him.

As we rode down a pink and gray cobblestone road, I looked at the leafless trees and patches of pine on the faraway mountains. This wasn't the winter wonderland I had hoped for. Instead of sparkling white snow, I saw brown grass and dead shrubs. It was as if everything was at the beginning of winter, after leaves had fallen and the cold nights had prevented new growth before the snow came.

Ethan rode next to me, with Cormac in front and Dane behind me, Tristan at his side. We were riding quickly enough that conversation would be difficult so I kept my thoughts to myself. Though I wondered if there was a way I could ask Tristan about the landscape here without offending him.

We rode parallel to the mountains, never toward them. Something inside me longed to visit those peaks. I'd never been on a mountain, but I'd learned about them in my limited geography lessons as a child. I knew well enough that there were mountains and oceans and lakes so wide that humans couldn't see across them.

All I had seen was either forest or grass or farmland. The

seasons changed back in the human realm, each of them bringing life or death in an endless cycle. It seemed odd to have these places nearly frozen in one part of that cycle. How did they ever grow crops in the Winter Court? If spring never came, they would never have the summer growing months for the fall harvest. I'd seen the Fae eat, they clearly needed food, and lots of it. Where did that come from? They couldn't have grown it themselves, could they?

The sun neared the midpoint of the sky, a faded white disk behind a mask of thick gray clouds. Cormac finally slowed and stopped. Ethan and I stopped behind him and Tristan rode up alongside. "Ready for break already? I assure you, the horses from the Winter Court ride all day and night. All creatures of the Winter Court can do that." Tristan grinned.

I shook my head and turned away from him, not wanting to indulge his innuendo.

"I'm concerned about Cassia, she's never done a ride longer than a few hours. She needs the rest," Cormac said.

I would never ask for a break, which I think Cormac knew. The thought of getting off the horse and stretching my legs was very appealing. "Maybe just a short one?"

Tristan was off his horse before anyone answered me and offered his hand to help me off of mine. "Why don't you stretch your legs then we can continue on. When we get to town, I'll show you some of the Winter hospitality we're so well known for," Tristan said.

I hesitated before taking Tristan's hand. I'd heard nothing but bad things about him and had applied those rumors to all of the Winter Court. Though, now that I was thinking about it, I'd been shown nothing but excellent hospitality. Unable to hide my smile, I took Tristan's hand.

WE PASSED homes settled off the road, increasing in number the closer we got to town. In the distance, I could see buildings crowded together. Wherever Tristan was taking us, it was the most densely populated place I'd seen so far in Faerie. The road widened as we approached the first grouping of buildings. Several carts and buggies pulled by horses passed us, leaving town as we entered.

We seemed to have arrived on market day. The streets were lined with tables covered in goods. Fruits and vegetables, pottery and housewares, fabric and jewels overflowed as various vendors shouted at passersby to gain their attention. The streets were lively, and full of people who ducked around us as we carefully made our way through.

There were more Fae gathered at this marketplace than I'd seen the night of the wedding. I looked around the town trying to discern its size. There had to be hundreds of buildings here and all that I could see seemed in good repair. Despite the desolate landscape, the Winter Court seemed to be thriving. Where they got the fresh fruit and vegetables from I didn't know, but they didn't seem to have any problems surviving in this cool climate.

Tristan stopped in front of a three-story building with large glass windows and intricately patterned brickwork. As soon as we stopped, someone came through the door and greeted us with a sweeping bow.

I expected to see another blue clothed servant, but this Fae male was tall and dressed in a crisp white tunic and gray leggings that looked like something I might find Tristan himself wearing. The Fae who greeted us had the same glowing quality every Fae I'd come across had. His bright blue eyes and strong jaw line quickly caught my attention. He didn't look like the guests at the wedding. He looked more like my princes and with his long blond hair he could be mistaken for Tristan's brother.

Tristan dismounted and offered a hand to me. I took it and climbed off the horse. The man who had exited the building stood waiting calmly, hands clasped in front of him. As soon as I was off the horse, Tristan guided me over to him with his hands on my shoulders.

The man bowed. "Welcome, My Lady, Your Grace."

"No reason to be so formal, Kai. She's a friend not a fucking dignitary."

"Some of us in the Winter Court have manners," Kai said. "May I take your cloak?"

"Such a show off, this one," Tristan said with a grin. "Kai, this is Cassia. Cassia, my cousin, Kai."

Kai inclined his head. "Lovey to meet you, Lady Cassia. And more friends who aren't dignitaries?" Kai lifted an eyebrow and I turned to see what he was staring at.

Ethan, Dane, and Cormac had joined us at the front entrance to the building.

"Yes, friends," Tristan said. "For now."

"Come on in, your suite is ready for you," Kai said.

Tristan walked in through the double doors and I followed close behind him. I was grateful that Ethan, Dane, and Cormac were right behind me.

I looked around the massive formal entryway. Gray marble floors stretched in front of us, capped by walls covered in white damask wallpaper. Along the wall on either side were pedestals topped with small sculptures. One wall held a massive tapestry showing a battle scene. Masses of bodies punctuated with bursts of red. I turned away from it and looked at the other wall where a series of framed paintings showed portraits of Fae males who all looked very similar to Tristan and his cousin, Kai.

"Will you all be staying with us this evening?" Kai asked.

"They're all staying," Tristan said. "Will you please prepare the guest rooms?"

Kai nodded, then walked down a wood paneled hallway and disappeared out of sight. I turned and looked at Tristan. "What is this place?"

"We call this place the Small Palace. It used to be the primary home for my family, but we outgrew it. Kai runs things for me in this part of the Winter Court, so he lives here."

That was more of an explanation than I was used to getting from any of the other princes I'd been traveling with. I wondered if I could press my luck. "So why is the Winter Court separate from all the others? Why did you leave during the war?"

"I think that's enough history for today," Cormac said.

"You can't keep her sheltered forever," Tristan said. He offered me his elbow. "Why don't I give you a tour?" He glanced back at the other Fae. "Don't worry, Kai will show you to your rooms shortly. And I'll bring her back in one piece."

I felt like I was being pulled in two directions. Behind me, the princes had saved me countless times. Dane and Ethan who I'd been intimate with and Cormac who I fantasized about being intimate with. We'd known each other such a short time yet they already felt like they were part of me.

I hesitated next to Tristan, working up the willpower to follow him. I wanted to hear what he had to say and I was curious about what insight he might offer. He might come across as cold and impersonal, but he was the only one of the four who easily answered my question.

"Don't worry, I won't bite unless you ask me to," Tristan said, a wicked grin spreading across his face.

I glanced at his teeth and caught sight of his sharp canines. Fae teeth were definitely more predator than human. I knew I should've felt fear from that glint in his eyes. He was trouble and I knew it, but I couldn't stop myself. I threaded my arm through his waiting elbow, and without a goodbye to the others, I followed him down the hallway.

## Chapter Three

"These used to be the servants' stairs," Tristan said as we walked single file up a narrow, dark stairway. "Things were different when we were all part of the same kingdom. Servants in most Courts are expected to be invisible at all times. Here, it's a job. They're paid for their time and granted equal representation as a citizen."

"I saw the servants at Cormac's home and at a wedding we stopped at in the Autumn Court," I said.

"Cormac's father must be visiting the Queen then," Tristan said.

Tristan waited for me at the top of the stairs and I joined him in the hallway. "What do you mean?"

"All servants in Faerie belong to a different kind of Fae. They are Brownies, helper faeries. They don't have the same kind of magic as the High Fae, which all of the ruling class are. Which, I guess you are."

"My maid growing up told me I was a changeling before I fled the human world. She said she was a Brownie, and that she had been working for my mother," I said the words without really considering the meaning of them, or what Tristan might think.

He seemed to ponder me, his brow furrowed while he studied my face. "It's possible you're from a noble house then. While some of the merchant class can afford to keep and care for Brownies, they mostly serve the High Fae of the nobility."

"Then why did they send me away?" I asked.

"I don't know," Tristan said.

Not wanting to think about how hurt I felt, I changed the subject. "What do you mean by Cormac's father must have been away?"

"The Brownies in Faerie aren't free. They aren't paid for their work and they have no voice as citizens of the realm. It's one of the few areas in politics where Cormac and I agree. Neither of us believe they should be treated as less than us, but Cormac's father has a stranglehold on the old ways. I've heard the new Queen is more lenient with her servants, there's even rumors she pays them, but that doesn't mean they have a choice," he said.

I frowned, not liking what I heard. I knew the servants we had growing up weren't paid well, and I knew they had little voice when it came to matters of politics, but so had I as a woman. Politics was considered a man's domain in the human realm. Here, they had a queen. Maybe it was time for me to start paying attention to the things going on around me. It might be possible to have a voice in this realm. "Everyone should be free to make their own decision. And they certainly shouldn't be forced to work for anyone."

"I think you're going to rather enjoy your time in the Winter Court," Tristan said. He swept his arm toward the long, formal hallway in front of us. It was lined with plush red carpet and the walls were covered with striped silver and white wallpaper. Now that I knew this place used to be the primary palace of the Winter Court, the extra attention to detail made sense. I walked down the hall as Tristan had indicated and he followed one step behind me.

"This floor contains my rooms. No one else uses them so they are very private. Of course, you're welcome to stay up here with me."

I stopped and turned to look at Tristan as I pressed my lips into a tight line.

"In your own room with your own closed door, of course." Tristan put his hands up in mock surrender. "These are the chambers designed for the Prince and Princess of the Winter Court. So there are separate bedrooms that connect to sitting rooms, dining areas, and a library."

He opened the door and we stepped into a comfortable looking sitting room. A sofa and several chairs were arranged around a low table. Against one wall was a dormant fireplace. A few shelves held what appeared to be games and books. I wondered if Tristan sat in here alone playing cards or if this was where he brought and entertained females.

Tristan cut through the room, walking straight toward one of two closed doors. He opened the first door, then crossed the room again to open a second on the opposite side. "This door," he indicated the right, "takes you to the prince's room." He swept his arm to the left. "This room is for the princess. While we are here, it's yours to use. If you want it."

I had to admit, I was curious what a room designed for a princess looked like. Taking slow steps, I walked toward the open door and stepped inside. Just like everything else in this palace, the princess's room spared no expense. A four poster canopy bed was the centerpiece of the room sitting on top of a massive ornate rug that probably cost more than everything in my entire childhood home. A wardrobe, two bedside tables, and a circle of four chairs in the corner completed the furniture. The chairs were situated next to a large glass window framed by sheer white curtains. Directly across from the bed, trimmed in white stone with silver inlay, was the fireplace.

The walls were white wallpaper covered in a pattern formed by silver birds. Everything about the room was simple, understated luxury. It was clear it was all the best money could buy, and yet none of it was over the top.

I could feel Tristan standing behind me now, his warm breath on my neck. "What do you think?"

"It's beautiful."

"I imagine you'll sleep well here tonight," Tristan said. "And I'll be right across the sitting room if you need me."

"I don't know if I can stay here. I'm no Princess. I can stay in a guest room like the others."

"If you'd like to share with one of the males," Tristan said with a shrug. "You have to make a choice though, would it be Dane or Ethan? I suppose it could even be Cormac, maybe you're the one to finally thaw that icy soul of his."

My cheeks heated, but I didn't turn to look at Tristan. He had a point. If I slept near any of the princes, I would be tempted to crawl into bed with one of them. When I'd been with Dane, it felt natural and for the first time I didn't feel like I was letting anyone down or hurting anyone's feelings. Because it had just been him and me. When I did it with Ethan, the others were away. So I hadn't felt guilty, but now they were all here together and they might expect me to make a choice which was something I couldn't do.

How would I make a choice when the others would be watching me? I didn't want to offend anyone or be forced to make a choice. If being with one meant saying no to another, I wasn't sure I could do that. I didn't want to make a choice. "You'll let me sleep here, alone?"

Tristan inclined his head. "I'm not sure what your friends have said about me, but I don't force females to do anything they don't want to do. One day, you'll come to me. Until that time, I won't touch you."

I pressed my lips together into a tight line, trying to hide the rush of curiosity accompanied by a tingling between my legs. It wasn't fair that he had this kind of command over my body without even knowing me. I wondered if my reaction had to do with the things I did with Ethan. Had he awakened some dormant part of me that now wanted to have sex with every male I met?

"You should probably go back downstairs and find your males, I'm sure they're coming up with all sorts of imaginative things that the two of us were doing in their absence." Tristan turned and walked toward the main entrance to the suite.

I followed him out the door, still too confused about the strange feelings I was having for him to speak. It was as if something in me had changed since arriving in Faerie. I'd never had feelings like this for any human men and now I found myself lusting after four Fae princes. I hoped my visit with the Queen would help me figure out some of the confusion I was feeling.

Downstairs, I found Cormac pacing in the entryway where we'd parted ways. He stopped walking when he spotted me.

"Waiting to see if I violated her?" Tristan asked.

Cormac frowned. "Cassia, I'm sorry you have to spend time with him."

"If the Queen proves she's Winter Fae, she'll get to spend so much more time with me," Tristan said.

"We'll see about that," Cormac said. "Cassia, I promised I'd start teaching you." He glared at Tristan. "And I make good on my promises. Always."

The tension in the room was suffocating and all I wanted to do was separate these two. "Thank you, for showing me around, Tristan." I turned to Cormac. "I'm ready to learn whatever you have to share."

## Chapter Four

✦

Cormac secured us a place inside an empty stockyard. The smell of animals hung in the air of the large wooden building and the soft dirt ground was filled with divots and footprints from the previous inhabitants. I didn't ask how he knew about this place or how it came to be empty. I was grateful for the moment of peace and a place with a roof over us for training.

Outside, icy cold rain pelted the roof like thousands of tiny stones falling from the sky. I always associated snow with winter, though I supposed we got our share of cold rain as the seasons changed in the human realm.

"The first thing you need to know about being Fae, is how to channel magic," Cormac said. "Now, I won't be able to help you with all the magic you seem to have, but at least we can work on you keeping it contained so it only comes when you need it."

"That would be nice," I said. "So far, I've blinded people when I'm scared."

"Yes, you have done that. Believe it or not, that's a sign of some pretty powerful pent up magic," he said.

"When I learn how to channel, can I still do the thing with the light?" I asked.

"Maybe," Cormac said. "I'm honestly not sure. I've never seen anything quite like it, but I have seen others manifest unusual magic when they didn't know how to use it. The difference is, it's usually in children and we know Fae magic strengthens as you age."

"Do you really think I have magic from three courts?" I asked.

He pursed his lips as if trying to keep from blurting something out.

"What?" I asked.

Cormac sighed. "I think you have magic from all four. But I'm not sure yet."

My brow furrowed. "What makes you think that?"

"Mostly, it's the way the Sodalis tracked you. Uncontrolled magic is like an invitation to the monsters from the Under. It's part of why we have the Academy to train young Fae how to manage their magic."

"That can't be it, though," I said. "From what you've said, any magic could draw in the Sodalis. Why would you think I had four Courts?"

He shook his head. "You have some of the Summer Fae qualities."

"Like?" I asked.

"Your ability to talk your way out of things, for one," he said with a smile.

"I didn't know that was a Summer Fae quality," I said. "What else?"

"It doesn't really matter," he said. "We need to focus on helping you keep your magic under the surface so it doesn't call to any more monsters."

I wanted to know more about what he thought could be attributed to the Summer Court, but I knew Cormac well enough now to know he wasn't going to tell me anything he wasn't ready to share. Hopefully, the Queen would help me figure all of that out. For now, I needed to survive. Anything that would prevent me from having to encounter another Sodalis was something I could get behind. "Channeling it is. What do I need to do? I'd really like to stop being monster bait."

"The first step in challenging is control. You'll have to learn how to cycle your magic internally," he said.

I lifted an eyebrow, waiting for more explanation. The only thing I knew about cycling was the way farmers would rotate crops.

"When your magic is near, you feel it, I'm guessing," he said. "You feel it inside of you trying to break free."

I nodded. "I do. It's like something clawing at my insides."

He blinked, looking startled by my description. "Most people describe it as a tickle. Clawing?"

"It's definitely not a tickle."

"Well, that's probably because you have multiple courts worth of magic. Fae are only meant to have one kind of magic," he said.

"What about the Brownies?" I asked.

"They have their own kind of magic," Cormac said. "Not as powerful as High Fae."

"Is that why they're treated like slaves?" I asked.

"Who told you that?"

"Tristan," I said.

Cormac shook his head. "We're working on changing that. But now isn't the time to discuss politics."

I blew out a sigh. There was so much I wanted to learn, but I wasn't going to last long if I kept attracting monsters from the Under. If the monsters didn't get me, someone would eventually end my life as Angela had suggested to keep them from returning. "Alright. Politics later. Cycling now. Where do I start?"

"When your magic surges through you, it has to have a place to go. If you don't use it, it stays exposed. It can be sensed by the creatures from the Under," he said.

"That doesn't make any sense," I said.

"It's just how things are, Cassia," he said.

"No, not what you're saying. The fact that I even had magic at all. Nani, the Brownie who hid me, said changelings are stripped of their magic. How did I even have magic for the Sodalis to find in the first place?" I asked.

He shook his head. "I don't know. But then again, I've never met anyone who naturally had magic from all four Courts. It must have been too strong to stay dormant in the human realm."

"How did the Queen get hers, then?" I'd been wondering for a while how the Queen came to have the same magic that was causing me so much trouble.

"When a Fae wins Queen's Trial, she's given the key to the ancient temples. They hold the power of how one can wield the magic of all four Courts. It's difficult to contain and control, as you're learning."

"Why don't more Fae go to the temples to gain the power?" I asked.

"It's dangerous," he said. "Raw, left unchecked, like yours, the magic could consume you. If a monster doesn't get to you first. Plus, it's well protected. We can't have that amount of power falling into the wrong hands."

I took a few steps away from Cormac, blood rushing to my ears filling them with the rapid beat of my heart. "You never said anything about the magic consuming me. You only told me about the monsters."

"I didn't want to scare you," he said.

"Trust me, I was already scared of the Under," I said. "Now you're saying it's possible the magic I have inside could be just as dangerous?"

"Listen, you survived the Sodalis. That proves that you're strong. I can't teach you how to use the magic, but I can teach you how to keep it from sending signals to the monsters as to your whereabouts." Cormac's brow furrowed in concern. "I can help you contain the magic, keeping you - not the magic, in control."

I shook my head and looked down at the dirt floor. I'd felt so much lighter after the Sodalis were killed. I thought my next hurdle was simply about meeting the Queen and getting some help. I didn't realize the magic I held was so dangerous. Before I came to Faerie, I was mourning my freedom as I prepared for a wedding to a stranger. In the last few days, I'd had glimpses of hope. Moments where I thought that things might improve. That I might have the freedom and belonging I longed for. Instead, it seemed the deeper I went, the less choices I had.

Lifting my chin, I tensed my jaw as I stared at Cormac. I hadn't gone through all of that to give up now. "Show me how to cycle."

His lips turned up in a smile. "You can do this."

I smiled back. "I'm ready."

Cormac placed both of his hands on his heart and inclined his head toward me. I followed his example, placing my own palms flat against my chest.

"Breathing is the most important thing to learn to control when cycling magic. Maintaining control of breath helps to guide the magic where you want it to go." He took exaggerated breaths in through his nose and blew them out through his mouth.

I felt ridiculous, but I followed what he was doing, keeping my focus on his dark eyes. He matched my gaze with unflinching intensity and I felt flutters in my chest again.

"Do you feel your magic flair when you're scared or angry?" he asked.

"Yes," I said. "But not all the time. It seems to have a mind of its own."

"Part of that is your mind. When you maintain calm and keep your breathing even and your mind focused, you keep the magic from rising up. Once it flairs, it has to be used. You won't be able to send it away. So this tactic, cycling, is to keep the magic simmering just below the surface. It's strategic. If you ever need your magic, you want to release it at the right time, not waste it," he said.

"That's it?" I asked, dropping my hands. "Just breathe and focus?"

"Not quite," he said. "Those are the keys. The final step is to catch the start of the flair and tie it off."

My brow furrowed. None of the magic I'd seen or felt was tangible. It wasn't too different than the knots and flutters I felt in my gut and I knew I couldn't grab a hold of those. How was I supposed to do what he asked?

"It must all seem so strange," Cormac said, his voice soft and calming. His posture relaxed and he reached for me, then lowered his hand.

I found myself aching for that unfinished touch. Why did he keep so far away from me? I knew he'd been hurt, but he had to know I wasn't going to do the same things Angela had done, whatever they were. "Cormac."

He cleared his throat. "We should get on with it, the others will be wondering about supper soon."

My brow furrowed and I opened my mouth to say something, but wasn't sure what to say. There seemed to be so much unspoken between the two of us, but that didn't make any sense at all. I closed my mouth and nodded then wondered if I'd ever have the ability to translate these strange feelings for him. And if I did, would I be brave enough to tell him what they were?

"Magic is inherent in Fae so we feel it pulsing through us almost all the time. The flair up is when your magic is about to break free. To tie it off, you have to find the pinnacle of your power. This might take some work, and practice."

"How?" I asked.

"Close your eyes," Cormac said.

I obeyed.

Warm hands pressed against the sleeves of my tunic as Cormac rested his palms against my upper arms.

I could feel him in front of me. I could smell citrus and cedar, the scent that enveloped Cormac at all times. I could feel his warm breath on my neck as he whispered in my ear, "Search for the source of the light you create. Imagine you are inside your head, then travel down to your neck, your shoulders, your chest, your stomach..."

He continued to speak, but my breathing was heavy now and I couldn't focus on his words. All I could feel was the heat of his body so close to mine and a rising desire that I wasn't sure I could contain. "Cormac."

Fingertips traveled down my arms, sending a shiver through me.

"Cassia, I..." he hesitated, then his fingers left my skin.

My eyes snapped open and I stared at him, bitter disappointment making my chest tighten. Why did he stop?

"Well, well, well," Tristan said. "So this is where you're hiding my guest."

# Chapter Five

Embarrassment and anger surged through me in a twisting mess. Tristan strolled into the stock yard as if he owned the place. For all I knew, he did.

"And here I thought the honorable Cormac would actually be working on a training session. I should have known you weren't as pure as you pretended."

I could almost hear something snap in Cormac.

He charged Tristan, throwing all his weight onto the startled Winter Prince. Tristan landed on the ground, a cloud of dirt enveloping him like a halo. Cormac landed a punch on Tristan's face before the other male managed to scramble away from his assailant.

"Cormac!" I screamed. "What are you doing?"

Cormac stood, shoulders heaving with heavy breaths as he turned to face me. "I'm sorry you had to see that."

Tristan stood and dusted the dirt off of his white tunic. "How long have you wanted to do that, Cormac?"

"What is going on here?" I asked.

Cormac turned away from me, focusing his attention back on Tristan.

The Winter Prince was smiling and extended his arms wide. "I'm right here, Cormac. Get it over with. Everything you've dreamed about doing to me. Now's your chance."

"Stop this!" I shouted. "Both of you."

"I should," Cormac said, ignoring me. "I should make you feel the pain she felt before she died."

"Trust me," Tristan said. "There's nothing you could do to me that would hurt me worse than her death did."

"You were supposed to protect her," Cormac said, his voice low.

"You're right." Tristan lifted his chin toward me. "Why do you think I'm going along with you on this visit to the Queen? You have this changeling under your protection. It's not Lena, but at least I can honor her memory by helping you."

Cormac's hands tightened into fists and I worried he was going to charge Tristan again.

I stepped over to him and gently rested my hand on Cormac's upper arm. "Please, talk to me."

His jaw clenched and he took a deep breath before turning to look at me. "I'm sorry you had to see that."

"I don't understand what just happened." I looked over at Tristan, then back to Cormac, hoping someone would explain the reason for the fight.

"Cormac, I don't know how many times I can tell you this. She was my true mate. We loved each other."

"Then you should have protected her," he said.

"Yes, I failed," Tristan said. "Don't make the same mistakes as me."

I wanted to ask for more details, but both males looked so upset I was afraid to say anything.

After several moments of heavy silence, I felt the weight of Cormac's hand on my back. "Let's go. The others will be waiting for us."

"You can't protect her from everything," Tristan called after us.

"I can try," Cormac said as he guided me toward the door.

I looked back at Tristan and caught a momentary glance of him looking completely exposed, but it didn't last. He winked at me, his usual cockiness back in full swing.

Turning away from Tristan, I followed Cormac out of the stock yards and into the street. The cold of late evening hitting so hard it nearly stole my breath. I crossed my arms over my chest in an effort to stay warmer. Despite the long sleeves of my gray tunic, cold had settled into the Winter Court. I wondered why I hadn't felt it before.

Cormac seemed preoccupied during our short walk back to the Small Palace, not even noticing the puddles on the ground in front of him. I pushed him away from the water so he didn't soak his boots and he kept walking, not even acknowledging my action.

I frowned. Cormac was sullen and often in his own head, but this seemed worse than usual.

When we arrived back at the palace, Ethan and Dane were waiting for us in a small sitting room. Both males stood when we entered.

"How did it go?" Ethan asked.

"I'll be in my room," Cormac said, pushing past the two other princes.

"Cormac," I said. "Don't."

He didn't stop.

"What happened?" Ethan asked.

"Were you that bad at cycling?" Dane asked.

I heard the door open behind me and turned to see Tristan enter the room. Hand on my hips, I narrowed my eyes at the Winter prince. "What happened back there? What did you do? And who is Lena?"

"Lena?" Ethan said.

"You brought up Lena?" The summer prince took a few steps toward Tristan and I could tell he was looking for a fight.

I turned and put my hands on his chest, pressing into the firm muscles under his tunic. "Stop right there. No fighting."

Releasing Dane, I looked at all three males in turn. "One of you better start talking. No more secrets. If we're all going to be traveling together and sleeping in the same places, I can't be the only one who is in the dark here."

Silence hung in the room and I wondered if I'd pushed too hard. After all, they were all royalty and I was just a foundling Fae they rescued. I had no right to demand anything of the males who had saved my life and were now helping me figure out how to stay alive.

Just when I was going to relent and apologize for being so harsh, someone spoke.

"It was a long time ago," Tristan said. "Before the Winter Court split."

"What was?" I asked, gently.

"The current Queen is from the Autumn Court," Tristan said. "Prior to her rule, our Queen was of the Winter Court. Which made high families in the Winter Court desirable for alliances."

"His sister was the Queen," Dane added.

"What?" I asked. "But your father rules the Winter Court. Your court left Faerie."

"After her rein ended. It's complicated," Tristan said.

"Get to the point," Dane said.

"The point," Tristan said. "Is that my heart was broken and yet, your friend, still can't find it in him to forgive me."

"We all know it's your fault she died in the Under," Dane said.

"Who?" I asked, then I looked over at Dane. "Please, let him tell the story."

"Thank you, Cassia," Tristan said. "Lena, my mate. She believed that we could strike a deal with the creatures of the

Under to prevent them from terrorizing us. She went to the Under to find their ruler."

My insides twisted. I knew where this was going. "Why didn't you stop her?"

"You sound just like Cormac." Tristan managed a weak smile. "Tell me, if it were Cormac who was going to the Under, do you think you could convince him not to go?"

"No," I said without hesitation. Cormac was not someone you could talk out of things.

"His sister was just like him," Tristan said.

"Sister?"

"Yes," Tristan said. "He still blames me for her death." He glanced at Dane and Ethan. "They all do."

"So that's the reason for your bad reputation?" I asked.

"Oh no, that's justified," he said. "But I can assure you, all of my playmates have been willing participants."

I didn't understand why Cormac was still hanging on to this. If his sister had been anything like him, even Tristan wouldn't have been able to stop her if she put her mind to it. But now that I knew some of the background between the two males, I understood why Tristan was so willing to help me. "Are you really doing this to make it up to Cormac?"

"He'll never believe me, but I loved his sister. Even if it was an arranged marriage. I wasn't able to protect her the way I should have so he'll have to settle for you," he said.

"So you're trying to make it up to him?" I asked. "Why do you care?" I asked, feeling awful for saying it. The Winter Court was at odds with the rest of Faerie. It made no sense that Tristan would care.

"Because they used to be friends," Ethan said. "We all were."

"The Spring Prince is right," Tristan said. "But I'll never admit it again."

I frowned. All the effort of looking like a bad guy was all for show. I wondered what the real Tristan was like. I felt like I'd caught glimpses of what he might be behind closed doors. For a moment, an image of Tristan shirtless, sitting in front of a roaring fire flashed before my eyes. The shadows of the flickering firelight made his muscles stand out even more, accentuating his wash-board abs that led down to his sharp hip bones. He was wearing trousers, but they left little to the imagination. In the vision, his strong arms wrapped around me and I could feel the bulge of his manhood against my thigh.

With a gasp, I shook my head, sending the image away. I bit down on my lower lip, hoping nobody was able to see inside my head.

"Was it a vision?" Dane asked.

I shook my head. "It was nothing. I think I'm just hungry."

Tristan was staring at me, one eyebrow lifted in question and a half smirk on his lips. "You're welcome to eat in your rooms if you like, there's a very nice fireplace in the sitting room."

My jaw tightened. Of course he knew what I had seen. He might not be able to see my future, but I had a feeling he saw that vision as clearly as I had. "No, thank you. I'd rather eat with the horses."

"That won't be necessary," Ethan said. "There's a tavern down the street. We should be in time for supper."

"You three have fun," Tristan said. "In case anyone is looking for me later, I'll be in my room. You remember the way, don't you, Cassia?"

I ignored his comment and tried not to think of what Tristan looked like with his shirt off, skin glistening with sweat. Tingles danced between my thighs and I silently cursed my traitorous body. As soon as Tristan turned and walked down the long hallway, I turned away from him.

Tristan might not be the bad guy I painted him to be, but I was already deep enough in with Ethan and Dane. I didn't need to throw another prince into the mix. I already felt guilty enough as it was for being with both of them even if neither of them seemed to have a problem with it.

"Ignore Tristan," Ethan said.

"As soon as we get you to the Queen, he'll have to come back here," Dane said. "No way she'll allow him to stay."

"Why do you all speak so ill of him?" I asked. "He doesn't seem so bad."

"He wasn't once," Dane said.

"I'm afraid the loss of Lena hit him harder than anyone guessed," Ethan said. "He acted out in ways unbecoming of any Fae, royal or not."

"He said it was an arranged marriage," I said. "I thought you said Fae mated. That it was destiny that brought them together."

"It is, most of the time. Occasionally, in the elite houses, arrangements are made as they are in the human world. But it's rare," Ethan said.

"Extremely rare," Dane said. "And selfish."

"Cormac's father wanted power so he offered his daughter as bride to the Queen's family. Tristan's father took him up on the offer and the two were wed," Ethan said.

"How long does your father control your life here? Do you ever gain your independence?" Immortality seemed an awful curse if you never had any say in how you lived your life.

"For females, it's all about Queen's Trial, for males, it's different," Ethan said.

"How?" I asked.

"Females are eligible for Queen's Trial when they turn twenty and they remain eligible until they are fifty. After that, they are no longer under their parent's watch," Ethan said. "For males, you never really lose that connection if you want to inherit the lands. Oldest child has it the hardest."

"That's why I enjoy being the third son," Dane said. "I get the title and the parties, but none of the work. My brother, Stephan on the other hand, doesn't have it so good. He'll stay in the

Summer Court to learn from our father until he takes over the position as the Summer Minister."

"What about you, Ethan?" I asked.

"I'm the second born, but first son. However, my sister did not pledge to Queen's Trial so she can inherit the title of Minister," he said.

I felt dizzy with all of the new information spinning in my head. There was so much to keep track of and so many rules. It might take an entire human lifetime to learn it all. I'd always avoided discussions of social politics with my father. I understood the basics, but there were nuances I never grasped. I'd always found it rather petty and dull. Trying to climb higher than his status had cost my family nearly everything and was constantly on my father's mind. He never seemed to slow down enough to enjoy his life. I didn't want a life like that. I wanted to be happy with the simple things.

We stopped in front of the tavern and Ethan opened the door for us. I had to admit, learning about the politics and life of Fae royalty wasn't as exciting as running from a Sodalis, but I would listen to these two talk for the rest of my life if it meant I got to avoid seeing one of those drooling creatures.

Settling in to a cozy corner table between Ethan and Dane, I felt the tension I'd been carrying melt away. It didn't matter what we were talking about. As long as I was with them, I was happy.

I was worried dinner would be awkward with Dane and Ethan, that I'd have to explain myself or that one of them would try to assert their right to have me. I couldn't have been more wrong. As the friendly Brownie server brought out cups of ale and soft, brown bread, Dane caught us up on the details of the Sodalis hunt that Ethan and I missed out on.

"There were at least twenty of them," Dane said. "But once we got through the first few, they couldn't get back through that tear fast enough. The vultures had a feast that day."

I lowered the bread I was about to eat and set it on the plate in front of me. "Could we talk about something that isn't going to make me lose my supper?"

"Sorry, love." Dane's hand found my thigh under the table and he gave a gentle squeeze.

On my other thigh, Ethan was resting his hand, unmoving. There was something exciting about having both of the males I was involved with touching me in public. Nobody else could see, but I could almost hear my human mother chiding me.

The server returned and set two steaming bowls of stew on our table. "I'll be right back with the last bowl. Want more bread here?"

"Only if you're the one that brings it," Dane said, winking at the female.

She stifled a giggle as she turned away from our table.

"Why do you always do that?" I asked.

"Do what?" he asked as he slid the bowl that was in front of him to my place.

"Flirt with every female you meet," I said, picking up a spoon. I wasn't going to turn down food.

Dane's brow furrowed and he looked like he was considering the question carefully. "I'm not sure, really. Must be that I like females." He shrugged.

Ethan leaned closer to me. "Must be that he hasn't met the right one yet."

Dane's grip tightened on my thigh and my eyes widened in response. "Dane!"

"Sorry." He lifted his hand and set it on the table.

"Here you are, dear." The brownie set down a steaming bowl of stew and a fresh loaf of bread in front of Dane. "I had them give you an extra scoop."

"Thank you, doll," he said, flashing a toothy grin.

She giggled again as she turned away from our table.

I turned to look at Dane, eyebrows raised in surprise. "You can't turn it off, can you?"

"Well, I couldn't exactly wink at her once and then ignore her," he said.

"You don't have to ignore a female to be nice to them," I said.

He lifted a huge bite of stew to his mouth and made a show of chewing.

I shook my head and returned my attention to my food. I knew it shouldn't bother me to see him flirting with the server, but it did. I had no claim on Dane, but I found as we sat there, eating our stew in silence, I wanted to.

I knew I wasn't going to be sleeping alone tonight. But I wasn't going to be sleeping in Tristan's princess suite, either.

## Chapter Six

✦

When we arrived back at the small palace, I was surprised that Cormac wasn't waiting to greet us. He was apparently angry enough at Tristan to avoid being in any of the common spaces. "Should we check on him?"

Ethan and Dane both shook their heads. "Just give him some time. He gets this way every year on Lena's birthday."

"It's her birthday today? And Tristan pulled that?" I marched down the hall to the back stairs before either of the males could stop me. Ignoring their calls after me, I climbed the stairs that I knew would take me to Tristan's rooms.

The splendid sitting room was vacant and now that I was standing in it, I realized I hadn't stopped to think about what I was going to do when I saw him. Slowly, I walked toward the closed door of Tristan's bedchamber and lifted my hand to knock. Hesitating, I wondered if I should turn around and walk away.

The door swung open, making the decision for me. Tristan stood at the doorway, completely naked. Head to toe, nothing covered, naked.

"What are you doing?" My voice came out shrill and squeaky.

He smiled. "I'm in my bedroom, preparing for bed. The question is, why are you outside of my bedroom at this hour?"

"At this hour?" I asked. "It's barely past dinner, it's a perfectly respectable hour." My eyes drifted downward, exploring Tristan's chest, defined abs, and surprisingly large manhood. My cheeks heated.

Forcing my eyes to return to his face, I tried to remember why I was here. "You are awful. Why would you taunt Cormac about his sister on her birthday?"

"I didn't taunt him," he said. "You were there. He attacked me."

I blew out a breath of frustration. "You're a child."

"As you can clearly see," he gestured to his now slightly erect member, "I am not a child."

"Can't you put on some clothes?" I asked.

"I thought you were here to live out that vision you had. Or is it not time for that yet?"

My jaw dropped open. "That is not going to happen."

Turning on my heels, I spun away from Tristan and walked toward the door.

"Any time you're ready, Cassia," he called after me.

Shaking from embarrassment and anger, I walked back down the steps and back to the sitting room where I found Dane waiting for me. "Where's Ethan?"

"He went to see to the horses since Cormac is disposed."

"Good," I said. I walked over to Dane and tugged on his tunic, forcing him to lower his face. Then, I pressed my lips against his.

Dane wrapped his arms around me sliding them down my hips and under my butt until he picked me up and pulled me closer against his chest.

I wrapped my legs around his waist and pressed my lips harder into his. He walked forward, carrying me while he matched my kiss with hungry pressure. I nipped playfully by his lower lip and he growled, then pinned me against the wall.

He broke the kiss and stared at me. His breaths coming out shallow. "You sure you want to do this? Because this time, I'm not going to be able to stop. I've wanted you since we first met."

My breath came out quick and shallow and I stared hungrily into his hooded eyes. I could tell the same desire that had turned my blood boiling was rising in him. "I don't want you to stop. I want everything."

Dane pressed his mouth against mine again, finding a rhythm with my lips. As he adjusted his grip on me, he pressed me closer as he pushed me harder against the wall. I could feel the bulge in his trousers pressed against my rear and it sent a thrill through me.

I was hungry, starved for physical attention, and tonight it seemed only Dane could satisfy me. I ran my fingers through his hair and he caught my wrist, pinning it against the wall. He pulled back leaving my lips wanting, while his intense icy blue gaze bore into my very soul. I whimpered, wanting nothing more than to feel the heat of his mouth on mine again.

One corner of his mouth turned up in a smirk and a second later he had me in his arms again, carrying me like a bride toward one of the closed doors in the hallway beyond. He hesitated a second at the door shifting my weight so he could reach the handle.

As soon as we crossed into the room he threw me onto the bed. The room was dark, curtains drawn and no lamps lit. The only light was from the crack underneath the now closed door. I heard the rustle of fabric and I knew Dane was stripping his clothes. I reached for the ties on my tunic and wondered if I should take my clothes off to be ready for him; but before I could make my decision Dane was on top of me.

In the darkness I could only make out shadows of the hard lines of his face and the ripples of his muscled form. I lifted my fingers and touched his temple, then slowly dragged them across his cheek and down to his firm jaw. My fingers trailed down his neck, over his sculpted shoulders and down the corded muscles of his arms before lingering on his hands.

I could hear his breathing, even and steady, almost in time with the beating of my heart. The bed creaked as he repositioned himself grabbing hold of me once again and rolling me on top of him. In a heartbeat, he had my tunic over my head and discarded it somewhere in the dark room. His hands were rough but comforting as they explored my naked body. They lingered on my waist before moving up to my breasts, caressing them and exploring every inch of naked flesh I had to offer. I was straddling him at his waist, but I still had a barrier of clothing between the two of us. It reminded me of our last encounter and I wondered if he was waiting for me to get one final confirmation that I was ready for him.

Reaching behind me, I felt his upper thigh and moved my fingers along until I found his erection. I took the shaft in my hand and gently wrapped my fingers around its girth. He let out a soft moan as I slowly moved my hand up and down, mimicking the movement that Ethan had made when he was inside of me. The skin was softer than I expected and as I continued to work my hand up and down, I felt the member grow even larger. Dane's breathing grew shallower and every so often he let out a satisfied moan. I smiled, feeling completely in control. There was something satisfying about being able to give him this much pleasure. After another minute, Dane sat up and in a quick motion threw me on the bed again.

"You have no idea the power you hold over me, do you?" he asked.

"I think I'm starting to understand," I said.

Dane's fingers tugged on the lacing that was holding up my trousers. He worked quickly and I raised my hips to help him as he pulled them down, undergarments and all.

It was dark, so I didn't feel as exposed by being naked laid out in front of him. But I had a feeling, I wouldn't have minded even if it were the middle of the day. I knew there was nothing wrong with what I was about to do. I had a connection with Dane, but I couldn't explain. It was different from how I felt about Ethan, yet with both males, I felt a need and a desire to be with them as intimately as possible.

Tingles of anticipation danced across my skin as Dane traced lazy circles on my stomach. He leaned down, kissing me along my waist, then my upper thighs, and finally kissing me at that most sensitive place between my thighs. I lifted my hips in response and moaned softly. His tongue flicked at the sensitive nub and tremors of ecstasy rippled through me, gaining in intensity with each passing second. I gripped the bedding, squeezing the quilt in my hands as I moaned again. My hips bucked and wave after wave of pleasure rolled through my body until they finally exploded in a crescendo of bliss. I cried out as the climax shook my core.

Dane lifted his head and I felt like I was sinking deeper into the bed as my body relaxed in utter and complete satisfaction.

"You ready for more?" Dane asked.

"There's more?"

"You're with a Summer Fae, love. That was just the warm up."

◈◈◈

When I woke the next morning, I knew the rumors about Summer Fae and Dane's reputation were completely deserved. In fact, more of my night had been spent stifling screams of ecstasy than actually sleeping.

"Good morning, love," Dane said.

I smiled lazily back, feeling completely content and at peace with the world in this moment.

Dane dragged his fingertips across my bare arm, gently caressing me before planting a soft kiss on my forehead. "I would ask if you wanted to go again before breakfast, but I've already heard several curious steps pause in front of our door. I imagine the others are wondering why we're still in here."

"Ethan," I said, his name off of my lips before I could stop myself. Guilt flared up in the pit of my stomach. Both for being with Dane and for saying another male's name while in his arms.

"He'll have to wait for his turn another night," Dane said. "Last night was for me and you."

"You won't make me choose between you?" I asked, still struggling to wrap my head around the nonchalant attitude that they had toward sex.

"I'll admit, sharing you might be difficult, but if that's what it takes to have nights like this, I'm willing to do it," he said.

"You're with girls all the time," I said. I leaned in and exaggeratedly batted eyelashes at him. "I'm sure you have nights like this all the time."

He growled at me playfully, then grabbed my shoulders, rolling me over. We tumbled to the ground in a tangle of sheets.

Laughing, I started to dig my way out of the bedding. Dane pounced on me, pinning me to the ground. "You're not getting away from me that easily."

"Maybe I don't want to get away from you," I said.

Dane lowered his face so his nose was practically touching mine. "You know you're not like other females. Now that I've had you, I don't know that any other will be good enough."

His words left me breathless, unable to respond. Coming from Dane, that had to be the highest compliment he could give a female. "Dane..."

He pressed his lips into mine, swallowing my words. It was as if he knew what I wanted to say even when I struggled to find the words. With Dane, words weren't how he expressed himself. His touch, his kiss, his body pressed against mine were all the confirmation I needed that he was falling just as hard for me as I was for him.

Sheets thrown to the side, Dane and I became a tangle of

flesh. It was as if we had both been starved and the other was our only source of sustenance. I gasped when he entered me, arching my back as his erection hit the spot inside of me that drove me wild. He held me close, my breasts pressed into his chest. The two of us were so close, it felt like we were one body. My fingers gripped his bare back as his thrusting sent me closer to the edge. I lifted my hips and dug my fingernails into him as I moaned, reaching my climax.

With a satisfied grin, Dane slowed down, but he wasn't ready to stop. He kissed the top of my shoulder, my collarbone, and my neck, giving me a moment to breath. Then, he lifted my legs so my hips were in the air and began to thrust inside me again. I gasped, as his erection nearly sent me to climax in a single thrust. Dane pressed on, and I grabbed hold of the abandoned sheets on the floor, squeezing the fabric in my hands as pleasure crashed through me in waves. Dane quickened his pace and I felt pressure building up inside me, begging for another release. Forgetting anything but the moment, I cried out, as the waves gave way to an explosion that made my thighs clench.

Dane finished, a tremor shaking him as he gently set my thighs back on the ground. Sweat glistened on his brow as he leaned forward. He kissed me again and stared at me with those blue eyes which were single-handedly capable of taking my breath away.

"I suppose we better put some clothes on. Or I'm going to have to keep you in bed all day with me."

The idea of spending an entire day in bed with Dane was delicious and enticing all too tempting. But I knew it wasn't possible. At least not now. We had things to do, and I knew his comments about people trying to listen into our room were probably true. I felt my cheeks heat. I'd probably been loud enough in the last few minutes to alert everyone in the small palace as to what we were still doing in bed.

Dane kissed me again before rolling off of me. He crossed the room and pulled on his trousers.

I moved a little slower, not wanting to return to reality. Finally, I forced myself to stand and started to look for my clothes.

Dane and I found our way to the dining hall where the others were already seated, being served breakfast by several servants. Remembering what Tristan had said about the servants in Faerie compared to the servants in the Winter Court, I lifted my hand in greeting to the first servant we came across, and to my surprise, the female Fae, who didn't look like a Brownie, greeted me back with a smile.

Most of the other servants I'd seen had shown very little emotion. It made me even more curious to learn about the politics and requirements of the way everyone was treated in each of the courts. I wondered if it was something I could study after I had my magic under control.

There were two available seats at the intimate dining table, one in between Tristan and Ethan and one next to Cormac. For some reason, I decided to take my chances next to the Winter Prince, and my other lover rather than sit next to Cormac. Once seated, I make quick work of filling my plate.

"It seems someone worked up an appetite last night." Tristan pushed a basket of sweet rolls toward me.

I ignored his comment, but took one of the offered pastries.

"It sure made sleeping next door to them difficult," Ethan said.

My cheeks heated and I knew I'd gone a shade deeper than usual in my blush and I looked up at Dane in horror. He was grinning like an idiot.

"While I do approve of sex as a tool for relieving stress," Cormac said, "getting some rest would have also been a good idea."

"Don't listen to them, love," Dane said. "They just wish they were the ones in the room with you last night. And they both know they wouldn't be able to make you scream the way I did."

"That's enough," I said. "I don't want to talk about this anymore. What I want to know is when we'll get to the Queen's Palace."

"Two days." Tristan looked over at Cormac. "And oddly, nothing has happened to Cassia so far."

"No more fighting," I said, knowing Tristan was just throwing more fuel on the fire. He'd said he thought Cormac was testing him, and at first, I wasn't sure what that meant. Now, I knew Cormac was waiting to see if Tristan harmed me. "I need all of you to help me with this and I'm not going to take sides."

Cormac stood, and I tensed, worried that he was going to shut me out again. Fear bubbled inside me and I opened my mouth to say something to change his mind. I didn't want him to leave me.

"I'll need Cassia for a training session before we go. She can't keep crossing in the open with her magic fully exposed. We don't need another attack from the creatures in the Under before we get to the Queen."

Relief washed through me and my shoulders relaxed. I closed my mouth and stood, without looking at the others. He was right, I didn't want any other monsters after me. Our last training session hadn't gone well, but I would have to figure out how to cycle my powers eventually.

Silently, I followed Cormac out of the dining hall.

# Chapter Seven

M y breath came out in clouds as we walked down the cold
Winter Court street. It was early morning and we
seemed to be the only ones up and moving around. The sun was a
sliver of light in the horizon, watery and muted. I was looking
forward to our return to the Autumn Court. The Winter Court
wasn't as wintery as I anticipated, but it was dreary and desolate
compared to the vibrancy and life of the Autumn Court. "Be
honest with me, Cormac." I tugged on the male's sleeve, halting
his progress. "Why aren't we just sliding to the Queen's Palace?
Why all the pageantry?"

He frowned. "We've been over this, Cassia. It's not polite."

"And we've been over this, Cormac. I don't like when you
keep me in the dark." I folded my arms over my chest and planted
myself in the middle of the barren road, trying to make it clear
that I wasn't moving until he talked.

His dark eyes trailed down my body, noting my stiff expression. With a noise that sounded almost like a growl, he dropped
his hands to his side in frustration. "I'm testing Tristan, as he
suspects."

I raised an eyebrow and didn't budge from my position. I knew there was more he wasn't letting on.

Cormac pursed his lips and studied me, warm brown eyes boring into mine, as if daring me to back down. I wasn't going to. Not this time. This wasn't life or death as it had been with the Sodalis, at least, not that I knew of.

"Fine," he said. "But not here. Come on." He turned and walked away, back to the stockyard where we'd had our first failed magic training session.

Releasing my arms, I jogged to catch up to him, trying not to smile too wide at the minor victory. Getting Cormac to share something of his plan was big. I knew he didn't even keep Dane and Ethan fully informed of everything. They just went along with him.

When we reached the back of the stock yard, Cormac slid the massive wooden door open and stepped into the open exterior. Soft dirt greeted my footsteps, a welcome change from the uneven cobblestones of the road. I shivered as Cormac shut the door. The open expanse of space might be enclosed, but it wasn't any warmer here than it had been outside. I turned to Cormac, eager to hear the information he was hiding. "So?"

He ran a hand over his dark hair, smoothing it back toward the braid he wore at the base of his neck.

For a moment, I wondered what his hair would look like free of its bindings, then I quickly shook my head to prevent any images of him from invading my mind. "What's the big secret?"

"I received a letter from an informant," he said. "Several of the high houses in the Winter Court called their soldiers in to report as soon as we arrived here. They're preparing for something."

I felt the blood draining from my face. I didn't actually expect his words to be as serious as this. Cormac came across as overprotective so often that I expected it to be something much smaller. I wasn't a prince or a warlord or anyone trained in military conquest, but I knew what it meant if the nobles were calling in their infantry. It wasn't something that was done lightly in the human realm. It always meant war. "Do you think they mean to attack Faerie?"

"I'm not sure yet," Cormac said. "But Tristan has never agreed to help us in the past and when it came to you, he didn't even put up a fight. He offered to join in our visit to the Queen even though Winter Fae haven't paid tribute to our Queen since the war."

"You think he's using me to get to the Queen?" I covered my mouth with my hand, feeling terrible for so easily inviting Tristan into our party.

"I'm not sure. But I needed more time with him before I take him into the Royal Court. He can't be trusted. I'm waiting for his true colors to show." Cormac took a step closer to me. "Can I count on you to help me with this?"

I lowered my hand and looked up at Cormac. "What can I do to help?"

"First, don't tell anyone about this," he said. "Second, keep letting Tristan think he has a chance with you."

"What?" I stepped away from Cormac, furious. "You want me to, what, flirt with him? Throw myself at him?"

Cormac's face turned as red as a beet and his eyes widened. "No, that's not what I want at all."

Crossing my arms over my chest again, I stared back at the Autumn Prince. "What then?"

"You turned down his offer to share his bedchamber, so he knows he's not getting into your bed," Cormac said.

"Of course he's not," I said.

"I want him to think he has your support. That you'll stand up for him as part of the party on our visit to the Queen."

My brow furrowed. "That's it?"

Cormac nodded.

I dropped my arms to my side. "I can do that. Now, show me

how to do this cycling thing so we can get out of here. The faster we leave this freezing wasteland, the better."

"I agree completely." Cormac walked to the center of the open space, then turned to face me. "Time for you to find the pinnacle of your power. If we can at least get you to isolate that today, we'll be in a position to work on cycling."

"Alright," I said, following him to the middle of the empty stockyard. I stopped and shook out my hands, trying to force myself to relax. Cormac's reasons for taking the scenic route to the Queen's Palace made sense and I wanted to show him that I was taking the threat seriously. Him opening up to me made me feel a surge of loyalty and could see why Dane and Ethan followed him so blindly. He might not always explain his reasons, but if he had a track record of making the right choices, it made sense that they wouldn't argue with him. Neither of the other males seemed to want the position of authority and preferred to follow. I wasn't keen on that but I'd help support an important cause.

Taking a deep breath in, I closed my eyes, settling in the most relaxed position I could get into while standing here in the cold. Ignoring the shivers, I kept my arms by my side, fingers spread wide.

"Clear your mind, try to let go of all your other thoughts. Focus on your magic," Cormac said.

I clenched my jaw, wanting to yell at him that I didn't exactly know what my magic felt like. But before I could say anything, I realized I did know. I'd been feeling it for a while. The clawing sensation inside me that threatened to rip me in two if I didn't let it free had to be my magic. It usually only showed up when I was in danger.

"It might take a while to find it, but it's there," Cormac said.

I opened my eyes and raised my eyebrows. "It's difficult to clear my mind with you talking."

"Right," he said, a slight pink flush rising on his neck.

I smirked, wanting to say something about the blush, but I

knew it was time to work. Closing my eyes, again, I felt a smile tugging at my lips as I recalled Cormac's brief embarrassment. I was sure he wouldn't appreciate being told how adorable it made him look.

Internally, I chided myself for letting my mind wander to Cormac when I was supposed to be thinking of nothing. The problem was, when you needed to shut off your thoughts, everything else went into overdrive. A hundred things seemed to buzz inside my head: A Sodalis chasing me on my wedding day, standing nearly naked in front of Ethan on the road, tumbling in between the sheets with Dane, and Cormac standing in a river with water dripping down his sculpted chest. I bit down on the inside of my cheek, trying to send the thoughts away, especially the vision of Cormac that had never happened. I was either fantasizing or seeing the future again. Neither would surprise me considering the fact that I was standing alone with the male, breathing in the faint scent of citrus and cedar.

Pushing the thoughts of the princes and monsters from my mind, I took another deep breath and focused on how I was feeling. My shoulders were tight and a little sore. My hips hurt from all the time spent on horseback or from all the time spent in bed. My thighs were a little sore from use, but it was a good feeling. As I went through an internal inventory of my body, I noticed a flicker in my gut that didn't feel right. Focusing on the feeling, I realized it resembled a less intense version of the clawing I'd grown to associate with my magic. Mentally, I tugged on the feeling, pulling at it to see where it would take me. A moment later, a flash of light that I could see through my closed eyes appeared and I was knocked to the ground.

Slowly, I opened my eyes and pushed myself up to sitting.

Cormac was bent over laughing. Through gasps of air, he said, "Looks like you found it."

I picked up a loose pile of dirt off the ground and tossed it at him. "Thanks for the warning."

He stood, shoulders still shaking as he chuckled. "To be fair, not everyone has that kind of reaction."

I stood and brushed the dirt off my trousers then put my hands on my hips. "Why does it feel like you thought I would?"

No longer laughing, but still wearing a smile, Cormac walked over to me. "It tends to have a stronger reaction for those with stronger magic. So it would make sense for it to happen to you." He brushed some dirt off of my back, his chest right up against my shoulder.

A different kind of flutter filled my chest and I pulled away from him, startled. Last time I felt like we'd connected, we'd been interrupted seconds later by Tristan.

Cormac lowered his hand and for a moment, a look of hurt flashed in his eyes, but it was gone nearly as fast as it appeared. He cleared his throat. "Well, that was successful. You've found your magic and now you know how it reacts to you reaching for it. We can do a few more exercises tonight when we stop to rest."

"That's it?" I asked.

"What else are you looking for?" he asked.

My heart thumped against my ribcage and I wanted to scream at him. What else was I looking for? I wanted him and he knew it. But he'd never make a move on me. He was going to make me work for it. I frowned, not in the mood to share my feelings first. "Nothing."

"Well, then, we better get going," he said, already walking away from me. "We've got a long ride ahead of us."

# Chapter Eight

W hen we returned to the small palace, Kai was waiting for us in the entryway. "His Grace has provided riding clothes for all of you and if you wish, a warm bath can be sent to your room."

I straightened in response to the offer of a bath.

"No time for baths," Cormac said.

I frowned. "We're going to see a Queen, shouldn't we be clean?"

"Yes, you should," Cormac said. "But you'll just find yourself covered in dust by day's end so it's a waste of time and water right now." He turned to Kai. "Please ask your master to ready the horses."

Kai inclined his head slightly, his jaw tense. "As you wish."

I could tell Kai wasn't thrilled to be get getting orders from Cormac, but it seemed that Cormac's status followed him to the Winter Court.

I was ready to leave the Winter Court behind, but I wasn't happy about skipping the offered bath. Baths were glorious. Especially the last one I had with Ethan.

As if he could tell what I was thinking, Cormac shook his

head and walked away from me. "Dress, we leave as soon as the horses are ready."

Cormac stormed off. Things were back to normal between us. I sighed and turned to Kai. "I don't exactly have a room."

"Aren't you with your mate, Dane?" he asked.

"Um." I wasn't sure how to answer that and a rush of guilt washed over me. I'd mostly shared Dane's room to avoid being so close to Tristan last night. I didn't regret a single second I'd spent with him, but I realized now that I hadn't made the decision rationally. I'd made the decision to go to him out of anger and the yearning of my loins. My cheeks heated. "He's not my mate."

"I see," Kai said. "Tristan will be pleased to hear that."

"It's not really any of his business," I said.

Kai shrugged. "Perhaps."

"Dane's room?" I asked again by way of ending the conversation.

Kai nodded.

I didn't stick around to see if he had anything else to say. Pausing in front of Dane's door, I knocked quietly before entering.

"Come in," Dane called.

I stepped into the room to a half-naked Dane and instantly turned away from him.

"It's not like you haven't seen it before, love," he said.

Dane was next to me now, his large hands on my upper arms. He kissed my cheek. "Those human habits you have are adorable."

He let go of me and I heard him walk away. I spun around, feeling foolish. Why had I turned away from him? Just a few hours ago, we'd been naked together. He likely knew every inch of my skin. Probably better than I did myself.

I glanced at the bed we'd shared and saw a pile of neatly folded clothes. All white and gray again as had become typical of everything Tristan offered.

Dane was wearing dark gray trousers and was pulling a lighter gray tunic over his head.

"I'm guessing these are Tristan's house colors." My mother growing up had been obsessed with our house colors. Her entire wardrobe reflected them. She'd grown up poor and throughout her marriage to my father, she'd gained wealth for the first time in her life. I don't even think her family had bothered to identify house colors when she was growing up. I always thought it was rather silly, but the simple act of wearing navy and ivory made her so happy I never argued it. "How do you feel about wearing them?"

He shrugged. "Doesn't matter. All clothes pretty much look the same once they're covered in dirt or blood."

I wrinkled my nose, not wanting to think about any of us covered in blood again. There had been too much of that on our travels prior to our arrival. "Do you think we have to worry about that again?" My voice wavered, showing my fear.

Dane's brow furrowed and he crossed the room to me, pulling me into an embrace. "No, love." He stroked my head. "No monsters this time."

I pulled slightly away from him so I could look up in his clear blue eyes. "How do you know? Cormac says my magic attracts them. I almost lost Ethan. I can't bear to think of what might happen if more of those creatures break through. I can't lose any of you."

"You won't," Dane said. "We've all dealt with worse than the Sodalis and we're all still here."

I buried my face into his chest, savoring the warmth and comfort of his embrace. When I was with any of the males, I felt safe and comfortable. I felt like I was home even in the middle of the Winter Court. I breathed in Dane's scent one more time before pulling away from the hug. "We should get ready to go."

Dane let go, but I could tell there was reluctance to do so. Could it be that the connection I felt toward him was mutual? I figured anything with Dane was going to be short lived based on his reputation. While I wasn't sure he'd ever settle down with anyone, including me, it was surprising to think that maybe he had real feelings for me beyond sex.

With that confusing thought in mind, I walked over to the bed and changed into the new clothes. They were thicker than what I was currently wearing. My trousers were dark gray and lined with something soft and thick. The tunic was white and thick like wool, trimmed in silver thread. A gray vest, lined with fur was left to go over the long sleeved tunic. I pulled the vest over the tunic, then sat on the edge of the bed to tug my boots back on.

The door swung open and Tristan stood in the door frame, his hand over his eyes. "You two decent?"

I grabbed a pillow off the bed and threw it at him.

He laughed and dropped his hand, then threw the pillow back at me.

I caught it. "We're just changing."

"Well, you might want to make your way to the stables. Cormac is getting restless," he said.

"And he sent you to fetch us?" Dane asked, eyebrow raised.

"Oh no, I sent myself. Thought I might be able to interrupt." Tristan smiled wide, showing his sharp canines.

I closed my eyes and let out a slow breath. *Two more days*. Tristan had a good side, I'd seen it, but it seemed after my rejection, he was back to being a cocky ass. I was looking forward to saying goodbye to him after we reached the Queen's Palace. That was, if nothing else happened along the way. My stomach twisted into knots and I recalled the conversation with Cormac. If Tristan was attempting something, he hadn't let on so far. But I trusted Cormac and if he believed his informant, I knew I had to be careful around Tristan. He couldn't be trusted.

Dane offered his hand and I took it and stood. Without a

word, the two of us walked out of the door, Tristan still holding it open for us.

I kept close to Dane as we walked out of the small palace toward the stables. Tristan walked alongside me, opposite of Dane, who was still holding my hand.

"You're going to see the heart of the Winter Court today, Cassia," Tristan said. "You might even find that you enjoy it."

"I doubt it," I said. "So far, the Winter Court has been cold, and inhospitable."

Tristan smirked, as if he knew I was talking about him more than the landscape. "You might be Winter Fae, you know. This could be your home," he said.

"It doesn't feel like home," I said.

"We'll see how you feel after today." He picked up the pace and walked ahead of us toward the stables.

Cormac was already there, holding the reins of two horses. As I approached, he held out the reins of one of the horses for me. "Do you need help?"

As much as I didn't want to ask for help, the horses of the Winter Court were too large for me to climb onto easily. I nodded.

I yelped as Cormac grabbed hold of my waist and lifted me with ease. That wasn't what I expected, but it was efficient. Quickly, he mounted his own horse. "Try to keep up," he called behind him. Then he looked over at me. "Ready?"

I smiled. He knew I could keep up. "Ready."

The two of us rode out onto the road, not waiting for the others to follow. I didn't care if he knew where he was going. I didn't care where we were going. The wind in my hair, the freedom of riding sent joy surging through me. Cormac glanced over at me and he looked just as happy as I felt. This was something the two of us shared: Our love of riding. Out here, on the open road, I felt like Cormac and I had an understanding, a connection that I didn't have with the others. This was how he communicated with me and for the first time, I truly felt like Cormac cared about me. I felt warm all the way to my core. How had I gone from unwanted bride-to-be to having the affection of three Fae princes? Even with the risk of monster attacks, I wouldn't change this for all the gold in the world.

# Chapter Nine

T he wind whipped through my hair as we continued down the well cared for pink and gray cobblestone road. All the roads I'd been on in the Winter Court so far, had the same flat stones on them rather than the depressed dirt roads of the Autumn Court. They seemed more luxurious covered in stones and I wondered if someone like Cormac would see it as a waste. He didn't seem the type to slow down and appreciate beauty.

The sky was a steely gray, and in the distance, I saw the outline of a watery sun. I wondered if it was like this all the time in the Winter Court or if they had days where they got real sunshine. One of these days, I might be able to start asking all of the questions that came to mind.

The farther we rode, the colder it seemed to get. Up until today, I hadn't felt this kind of temperature drop. My cheeks stung as the wind continued to whip around me and my fingers were starting to feel cold through the gloves. Cold seeped into my arms and legs, but thankfully, my chest was warm enough thanks to the extra layer of the fur-lined vest.

Cormac slowed his horse as we neared a fork in the road and I slowed mine to match his pace. As had become our habit while riding, Cormac and I took the lead while the others followed behind us.

"We'll need to wait for Tristan," Cormac said. It's been so long since I've been in the Winter Court, I'm afraid my directions are rusty."

Tristan seemed to know why we slowed down, and a moment later, he appeared next to me, slowing enough to wink at me as he passed by. He didn't stop to wait for instruction or engage in conversation. Instead, Tristan picked up the pace, surprisingly leaving both Cormac and I in the dust as he took the left fork in the road.

Tristan's increased pace felt like a challenge. I straightened in the saddle, and followed him to the left. As I rode, Tristan gained more distance on me. If I wanted to catch him, I'd need to go faster. I leaned down, and clicked my tongue, urging my horse to catch the Winter Prince ahead of us.

I heard Cormac call something after me as I pushed forward to catch up to Tristan. I glanced behind me, surprised to see that Cormac hadn't increased his pace to keep up with me. Suddenly, nervous flutters filled my stomach as the space between Cormac and I widened. At the rate I was going, I'd be alone again with the Winter Prince.

I shook my head, and refocused on the road ahead of me. Tristan hadn't done anything to harm me and Cormac wasn't that far behind. Besides, the thrill of riding this fast won over anything else. Cormac knew that better than anyone. I pressed on, ignoring the stinging of my cheeks as the wind rushed past me, enjoying the sense of freedom and the taste of the fresh air as I made my way down the road.

Ahead, Tristan had stopped at another fork in the road. How he'd gotten so far ahead of me, I wasn't sure, but I intended to catch up to him. As I approached, I slowed my horse, stopping next to him. Breathing heavy, I looked around and was just about to ask Tristan what he was doing when I noticed snowflakes gently falling from the sky.

Small, perfectly shaped white flakes landed on my shoulders and in my hair and on my nose. I leaned my head back to look into the steely sky, watching the flakes as they fell. I extended a hand and let tiny snowflakes cover my black riding glove. I could see the details of each one, different and delicate and cut like little stars that sparkled in the faded light of the winter sun.

"I thought you might like this," Tristan said.

I looked over at him and dropped my hand. "The snow?"

Tristan nodded. "I told you, we're going to the heart of the Winter Court today. The closer we get, the more of winter you'll see. This is the point where the snow begins to fall and I knew the others would race right through it without stopping to look at its beauty. I had a feeling you would appreciate it."

I extended my hand again catching more snowflakes and studying them. Tristan was right, the snowflakes were stunning. I knew he was also right about the way the others would react. They'd ride through, not stopping to relish the beauty of the slowly falling snow.

I looked up at Tristan again, confused by his back-and-forth behavior. One minute, he was doing something like this, being kind and sweet showing me there was a pleasant side to him. The next minute, he acted as if he didn't care about anyone. I still didn't trust him, but I had a feeling one side of him was an act. I just wasn't sure which side yet.

The others caught up to us, slowing down when they reached us. "Is something wrong?" Ethan asked. "Are you all right, Cassia?"

"I'm fine, thank you," I said.

"It's about to get very cold," Tristan said. "It's a good time to break out your cloaks before we reach the heart of the Winter Court."

No one responded to Tristan, but I watched them all reach into their saddlebags and pull out their cloaks.

"Here," Tristan said.

I turned to him to see an arm extended, with a thick gray cloak in hand. As if directed by my thoughts, my horse slowly moved closer to Tristan. I reached for the cloak, and wrapped it around myself clasping it at the neck. "Thank you." I pulled the hood over my head to keep my hair from getting soaked by the falling snow.

Tristan nodded and fastened his own cloak around himself. "Stay close. We can't afford to get lost out here." He pulled back on his reins and continued to the right this time, riding away from the rest of us.

Cormac looked at me. "You holding up all right?"

"Yes, thank you," I said.

He nodded them pulled up on his reins, following Tristan down the road.

"After you, love," Dane said extending his arm after Cormac. Ethan nodded. I knew the two of them would follow me, staying behind as they had on our previous rides together. I offered them a smile and then followed Cormac and Tristan down the road.

My cheeks burned as the cold wind whipped past us as we rode in the swirling snow. The small flakes grew larger the longer we rode, turning into fluffy clumps of flakes that stuck to my cloak and caught on my eyelashes.

First, the flakes flew off of my clothing, but the longer we rode the more of them stuck to me, melting into my clothes until the damp began to soak into my skin.

I shivered, pulling my arms closer to my sides and gripping the reins tighter. My fingers were aching, but I knew that meant I still had feeling in them. I'd learned about the dangers of the cold in the winters of the human realm, but I'd rarely experienced cold myself. On winter days when the snow came down, I was prohibited from going on rides. My minimal experience with cold only came from short walks to the stables and the time I spent caring for my horse before returning to my home to a roaring fire.

My teeth were chattering now and my ears hurt. I wondered how much longer we were going to ride in this and wondered if I should say something to the others. But I looked around and realized that even if I wanted to stop there was nowhere to go to get out of the cold.

Despite the fact that the road was well-maintained, we hadn't come across another village or set of homes. I hadn't even seen a farm since we left the small palace this morning. I wondered how long we'd been riding and searched for any sign of the sun. The white and gray snow clouds and swirling snow blocked any chances of me seeing it. I felt a little disoriented not knowing what time of day it was. With any luck, we'd be done riding soon and would be somewhere with a welcome fireplace.

A gust of wind blew the hood of my cloak off of my head and my hair blew in front of my eyes making it difficult to see. I slowed my pace, and pushed my hair away from my face before pulling my hood back over my head.

While the swirling snow certainly was beautiful, Tristan's prediction that I would enjoy the heart of the Winter Court was very wrong. There was nothing enjoyable about freezing in the middle of nowhere. Just as I was working on the willpower to ask the others to stop, I saw the hazy outline of something large in front of us.

I squinted into the distance, trying to make out the shape ahead. A few minutes longer and the outline of a massive wall came into view. I couldn't see anything beyond the wall. It was tall enough to block out whatever was behind it. I hoped it meant we were approaching a city and we'd find somewhere warm and dry to stop very soon.

The longer we rode, the sharper the wall became and I could

finally see what looked like the promise of an arched entryway. Riders passed us going away from the wall, followed by a few carts and carriages. The closer we got, the more traffic passed us. Many of the riders dipped their heads as they passed Tristan, possibly recognizing his house colors.

Finally, Tristan stopped in view of the grand arched entryway guarded by several Fae wearing black leather armor. I rode up next to him, my teeth still chattering. Tristan looked over at me and frowned. "You're freezing."

I glared at him as best I could, the ice crystals clinging to my eyelashes making him blurry.

"Come on," he said. "Through the gate. I'll get you warm."

I nodded and silently followed him toward the gate. As he approached, some of the guards who were slouching or leaning against the wall straightened and stood at attention. They lowered their heads in a bow as Tristan rode through the gate.

I followed behind him, the guards leaving their head lowered as I passed by, no doubt thinking I was part of his household due to the clothes he'd dressed me in. I wanted to look back and check to make sure the others were safely through the gate as well, but I was too cold at this point to make unnecessary movements. Once we were through the gates, Tristan stopped and dismounted handing his reins off to a few young Fae waiting in the corner. I wondered if they worked for him or if they were just part of the hospitality of wherever we were.

Tristan came alongside my horse and offered his hand to me. I was too cold to even consider if what I was doing was a good idea and I let him help me climb down from the horse. My legs buckled as soon as I hit solid ground and before I could fall, Tristan swept me up in his arms. He pulled me close to him, and I buried my head into his warm chest, surprised that he wasn't as frozen as me.

"Perhaps you're not a Winter Fae after all," Tristan whispered near my ear.

My teeth chattered as I burrowed my head farther into his warmth, unable to respond. If his warmth was typical of Winter Fae, I most certainly wasn't one. The cold of the heart of the Winter Court felt like it had penetrated my soul. I wondered if I'd ever feel warm again.

Tristan pulled me closer and continued walking. I wasn't sure where he was taking me, but at this point I had to hope his intentions were pure. A few heartbeats later, we were inside of a building and Tristan set me on a bench. My fingers tingled as the warmth began to thaw my icy limbs. "Where are we?" I managed through chattering teeth.

"Safe. This is another house my family owns." Tristan started removing the laces from my boots and pulled them off one by one. Then he removed the cloak and the vest. "Can you walk?"

My teeth were no longer chattering and the snow ice crystals had melted off of my eyelashes. I wiped the moisture from my face with the back of my hand and looked up at him. "I think so."

He extended a hand and I took it, rising on unsteady legs. This time, I was able to take cautious steps without falling.

"There's a warm bath waiting for you upstairs, it will help get the last of this cold out."

I nodded. "Thank you."

He opened the door to a room where there was indeed a bath waiting in the center of the carpet. Steam rose from the large tub and I could already imagine what it would feel like to step my ice cold toes into the warm water.

"Do you need help undressing?"

I looked at Tristan, ready to make a snap comment, but he didn't look like he was mocking me. He was being genuine. Once again, showing me the nice side of him.

"No, thank you. I can manage."

Tristan backed away from me, toward the door. Pausing inside the threshold, he inclined his head. "Let me know if you need anything."

"Can you let the others know I'm here? That I'm safe?" I asked.

A split second frown crossed his face but he nodded. "I'll let them know. They're likely already waiting for us downstairs." He closed the door behind him and I heard his footsteps fade as he walked away from the room. Alone, and still recovering from the cold, I slowly peeled my clothes off, finding it more difficult than I expected with my sore joints. Finally free of the wet clothing, I inched my way to the warm water.

I dipped a toe into the steaming water, then stepped in. The feeling of pins and needles breaking my skin claimed the submerged foot. Powering forward, I stepped in with the other foot and clenched my teeth against this stinging of the water against my frigid skin. A few deep breaths later, and the pain subsided.

Slowly, I eased myself in until I was submerged up to my chest.

As I sat there, the warm water eased the chill that had seeped into my bones. I took a deep breath and sank all the way under the water feeling my nose and cheeks and ears stinging in protest at the contrast of hot and cold.

I came up for air and wiped the water away from my eyes and immediately screamed. A figure clad head to toe in black had one leg over the open window across from me and was pulling itself into the room.

I covered my chest with my arms and screamed again, backing into the edge of the tub. The figure charged me and panic surged through me. Before I could decide how to react, someone else came storming into my room through the door and charged my would-be assailant.

I heard running and the sound of fists making contact with bodies and watched the tangle of the two figures fighting on the floor. It took me a moment to realize my rescuer was Dane, who now had the upper hand. He knocked a weapon from my attacker before landing a blow across the assailant's jaw.

Someone draped something across my shoulders and I turned to see Ethan.

"Come on, let's get you out of here," he said as he gently lifted me out of the water. He dragged me away from the fight, wrapping a robe around me.

I couldn't tear my eyes away from Dane who was still fighting the mysterious stranger. "We have to help him."

I wasn't sure if I was even saying the words out loud as I struggled against Ethan.

"It's okay," he said. "You're safe, I've got you."

"Dane," I said. "We have to help him."

"Dane can take care of himself," Ethan said.

Just then, Cormac and Tristan ran into the room, the two of them pulling the black clad figure away from Dane. Cormac lifted my attacker and slammed him against the wall. "Who sent you?"

Tristan ripped the mask off of the figure's face and I gasped as I stared at a female who was glaring down at the princes with nothing but malice in her gaze.

"Who sent you?" Cormac repeated.

Something silver glinted in the light, catching my eye. She pulled a knife from somewhere on her person and was turning it in her hand toward Cormac. "Cormac! Look out!" I shouted.

She jabbed a knife at Cormac but Tristan wrestled it out of her grip before she made contact with anyone.

In a movement so fast I hardly saw it happen, Tristan sliced the woman's throat and tossed the knife aside. The dying Fae gripped her neck as blood surged through her fingers and ran down the dark clothing.

My knees gave way and Ethan eased me to the ground. I turned to him, not wanting to look at the gruesome scene anymore. Ethan cradled me in his arms, whispering words that should've brought me comfort.

Only right then all I could think of was blood everywhere and the dead, empty eyes of a female who had broken into the room I was alone taking a bath in. I'd had no weapon and I was completely unguarded.

My fear gave way to anger as I considered the events leading up to the attack. I'd followed Tristan in here blindly and he led me to this room and told me to take a bath. I'd been separated from my princes, cut off from my protectors and left alone and vulnerable. To top it all off, Cormac suspected that Tristan might try something.

I pushed away from Ethan and stood, wrapping the robe tighter around me. The bottom of the robe was soaking wet from the water of the tub, but the top was dry enough to at least give me some warmth.

Tristan and Cormac were in the corner standing over the body. Cormac leaned down and seemed to be checking the dead Fae for any identifying markers. Tristan straightened and turned toward me as I approached. "Did she hurt you, Cassia?"

Jaw tense, I marched over to him and slapped him across the face.

He touched his hand to his cheek and stared down at me in disbelief. "What was that for?"

"Was that you're doing?" I pointed to the dead Fae covered in her own blood. "Did you set me up? Is there some reason you want me dead?"

Color drained from Tristan's face and he shook his head slowly. "How could you think that of me? Everything I've done has been to help you." He turned and glared at Cormac. "This is your doing, isn't it? I try to help, and you poison her against me."

"How did she know that Cassia would be in here alone?" Cormac asked.

"Don't you think that if I wanted Cassia dead I would've done it myself on the first night while she slept in my palace?" Tristan asked. "You know me well enough to know that I handle my own dirty work. I don't pawn it off on others."

His words sent a shiver of guilt through me followed by shame for the accusation. He was right, he could've killed me easily many times.

Cormac leaned down and touched one of the buttons on the assassin's jacket, then he stood. "You're right, Tristan. I apologize."

Two soldiers walked into the room, then raced past me when they saw the body on the floor. They stopped in front of Tristan and bowed. One of them pointed his drawn sword toward the fallen figure. "How did she get in? We have guard station on every entrance!"

"She came in through the window," I said, pointing toward the curtains blowing in the icy winter breeze.

"That's impossible, all the windows are sealed," the soldier said.

"Then we have a traitor," Tristan said. "I need to meet with the captain of the guard. The rest of the house needs to be in lock down. Nobody move that body. Nobody in or out of this room, you got that?"

The two guards nodded. "Yes, Your Grace."

Tristan took a couple of steps toward me and paused to look me up and down. "You hurt?"

Shook my head, too embarrassed to speak.

"Good." Tristan walked away from me, followed by Cormac and Dane.

The look of betrayal in his expression made my heart feel like part of it had just shattered.

Deep down, I knew Tristan didn't want to hurt me. And all the questions I had about which side of his personality was authentic, seem to be growing into sharper focus. I wondered how much the cocky playboy was a mask to prevent him from being hurt again. Much in the same way that Cormac didn't let anyone get close, Tristan didn't want anyone to know deep down, he was brave, caring, and loyal. My lower lip trembled and I fought back against the tears. I made a mistake and I wasn't sure I'd be able to fix it.

# Chapter Ten

✣

"Cormac and Dane are going to keep a very close eye on Tristan," Ethan said. "I'll stay with you."

I was glad for his company, but it didn't help to ease the guilty feeling about Tristan. "This wasn't Tristan's doing, was it?"

Ethan hesitated and I turned to look at him, curious about his expression. His lips were pursed and he looked like he was considering his words carefully. "I'm not sure. But I tend to give the benefit of the doubt and in the past, it's gotten me in trouble."

"What do you mean?" I asked.

"When you look for the good in others, you'll find it. When you look for the bad, you'll find it. We're all a mixture of both. It's simply a matter of how you choose to act on your impulses."

"Are you saying you look for the good and ignore the bad?" I asked.

He shrugged. "I have on occasion."

"Whereas Cormac seems to look for the bad," I said. There was something sad about that, always looking at others as if they were going to let you down. Constantly waiting for them to betray you. I had trouble trusting, but not to that extreme. On the other hand, Ethan seemed to exist in a too perfect world, ignoring the fact that there were too many who could turn on you in favor of their own agendas.

"He didn't used to," Ethan said. "Cormac has a talent for reading creatures: animals and Fae alike. He used to be more even in his assessments. As time passes, he seems to err on the side of the bad rather than give someone a second chance."

"Because of what Tristan did?" I asked.

He shook his head. "He'd probably have forgiven Tristan if it weren't for Angela."

I sighed, knowing I wasn't going to get any more of that story. I'd been told before that it was Cormac's to tell and there was no way he was going to share that with me.

A gust of wind blew in through the still open window and I shivered. Pulling the robe tighter around me I realized I never thanked Ethan for being so thoughtful. If it had been up to Dane or Cormac or even Tristan to pull me out of the tub, I knew I'd still be naked. "Thank you," I tugged on the robe, "for pulling me out of the water and then keeping me warm."

"You're not warm anymore," Ethan said. "Come on, I'm sure we can find you something dry to wear in this place."

I tugged the robe tighter around me as I followed Ethan out of the room. Once in the hallway outside, I stopped walking and looked back at the still open window. "Should we close that?"

Ethan crossed in front of me and walked back into the room, passing the body of the fallen Fae, to the window. After he closed the glass pane, I heard a snap as a latch must have slid into place but I wasn't watching him. I was fixated on the dead Fae. "Why did they leave her there? Shouldn't they do something?"

"Tristan likely called his lead guard who will want to see the scene untouched," Ethan said. "I imagine they'll be here any minute."

Something shiny caught the light and I walked over to my assailant, stopping at her feet. The buttons on her coat were gold and glinted in the warm glow of the hanging candelabra. I knelt down and lightly touched one of them. "These are made with real gold."

Ethan joined me, kneeling at my side. He reached out and touched the button. "They are. That's unusual for anyone in the Winter Court. They don't use gold as it's associated with the Summer Court."

I tugged at the button and pulled it from her jacket, lifting it closer to my face. A pattern of flowers circled the round object. I handed it to Ethan. "Flowers."

He narrowed his eyes as he studied the button. "That's definitely not Winter Court."

I glanced up at the bloody neck of the female and instantly regretted it as bile rose into my throat. Quickly, I stood and backed away, turning toward the door.

As I arrived back at the door, Tristan and two guards met me in the hallway. Tristan frowned when he saw me. "You shouldn't be here." He looked over at the guard on his right. "Take her to one of the guest rooms, find her something suitable to wear."

"Wait." I wanted to tell Tristan I was sorry. The words seemed right on the edge of my tongue as I stared at his icy expression. His jaw tightened and I looked down, unable to meet his eyes.

"Just go, Cassia," he said.

I looked back up at him, my eyes finding his and wordlessly, I tried to let him know I regretted my actions. I still couldn't say it out loud, but I held up the button.

He took hold of the shiny gold object and studied it. "Where did you find this?"

"It was on the jacket," Ethan said before I could inject. "Solid gold and a floral design."

"That's not Winter Court," the guard on Tristan's left said, taking the button from Tristan.

"No, it's not," Tristan said, looking back at me. "And Cormac already informed me he'd found it. Maybe if you use some of those Autumn Court hunter qualities you'd find the pieces you needed to answer your own questions instead of making hurtful accusations."

"I'm sorry," the words came out in a whisper, guilt weighing on me like a sack of grain sitting on my chest. "I-"

Tristan held up a hand to stop me. "You should go, Cassia. We have a lot of work to do."

"If you please, Lady," the guard on the right said.

I looked at him and noticed he had a much smaller stature than Tristan or any of the princes and his skin had a slight blue tint. Was he a Brownie? Had the things Tristan told me about equality in the Winter Court been true?

"Ethan, I could use your help," Tristan said. "Cassia will be safe with Julian."

"Go ahead, Cassia," Ethan said. "I'll find you soon."

I tried to meet Tristan's eye once more before I left but he was avoiding meeting my gaze. My shoulders sank and I reluctantly walked over to Julian. Without a word, he began walking down the hall and I followed, forcing myself not to turn back to look at the Winter Prince I'd hurt so badly.

We walked silently down the carpeted hall. It was less adorned than the small palace. If not for the guards, I wouldn't even think this was a royal residence. "Where are we?"

Julian didn't respond. I sighed, unsure if it was an order to ignore me or if he hadn't heard me. With the way things were going today, either could be possible.

The hallway we were walking down was incredibly long, lined with doors on either side. I counted and added in the few doors we'd already passed. There were ten doors on either side. What kind of place would need so many small, closed off rooms?

A female scream sounded a few doors away from us and I froze, looking up at Julian for an explanation. Was there another attack? Terrified, I moved up against the wall as Julian pulled his sword from its sheath on his belt.

A door three doors away from us opened and a female holding

a bed sheet over her ran into the hallway. Behind her, what appeared to be a naked Orc ran into the hallway behind her.

The female ran to Julian and ducked behind him. "I told him I don't do that."

The Orc straightened, rising to his full height, head nearly touching the ceiling. "I don't come here to be disrespected."

Julian approached the Orc and the scared female moved against the wall next to me. She grabbed hold of my arm and cowered behind me. "Don't let him near me."

I glared at the Orc, furious at him for whatever he'd done to her. Then, I turned to the female and smoothed her white-blonde hair with my hand. "Shhh, it's okay. I'm not going anywhere."

She burrowed her face into my arm and sobbed gently.

"What did you do?" I screamed at the Orc.

Julian looked back at me. "Leave it, My Lady."

The female pressed against me sniffed and looked up at me, her eyes rimmed in red from tears. "Lady?"

I ignored her question and turned back to the scene between Julian and the Orc.

"You have two minutes to gather your things and leave," Julian said. "You're no longer welcome here."

"No. I paid for a whole night. I'm not going anywhere." The Orc snarled, balling his frying-pan sized hands into fists.

My eyes widened. There was no way Julian would be able to take on this Orc. I watched in surprise as Julian lifted his sword, prepared to battle the massive creature. Julian was much smaller than the princes I'd seen fight. And with this monster, I'd even be a little nervous for any of them.

The creature charged Julian and I turned away, not able to bare the sight of the naked Orc running down the hall. I'd take the dead Fae over a naked Orc any day.

The female next to me screamed again, a shrill sound that made me cover my ears. She clawed at my robe, grabbing fistfuls of fabric and holding tight. Her fear made me want to protect her and I fought against my own rising terror and held her in my arms, squeezing her so she'd feel supported.

Julian slashed his sword at the Orc and the creature roared but easily dodged the weapon. Then, he grabbed the sword, wrapping his meaty hand around the blade. Blood streamed from his hand, but he didn't seem to notice as he ripped the sword from Julian's grasp.

He tossed the sword aside. Julian stood frozen in front of the massive Orc, weaponless.

My heart thundered in my chest. This terrible naked Orc was after the scared female in my arms. The only thing that stood between us was a smaller than average guard.

The Orc lunged forward and grabbed hold of Julian with both of his hands, easily lifting him into the air. "I'm staying the night."

"No," Julian said defiantly. "You are leaving."

The Orc tossed his head back and laughed as Julian squirmed in his grip. Then, the Orc threw Julian down the hall, hard.

I heard the thump as Julian's body hit the ground five doors away from where the Orc was standing. He didn't move.

A mixture of fear and anger was making my blood boil. Tears threatened, but I wasn't going to let this monster win. That's when I felt it. The clawing inside. My magic wanted to come to play.

# Chapter Eleven

The magic rising inside me was comforting now that I knew what it was. I still didn't know how to use it, but it was possible if I could create a white light again that I might be able to blind the orc running toward us long enough for us to escape. I reached for the magic feeling it pulse and grow and respond to my thoughts.

Behind me, the terrified female screamed again but this time it sounded so far away. The only thing I could see was the Orc charging down the hallway. I braced for impact as I encouraged my magic to spill forward, taking any form it wanted so long as it would prevent the beast in front of us from reaching us. I wanted to stay back, I wanted to be afraid, but I knew I had to try to help.

Just as the first light surged forth from me, I felt someone familiar pass by. In the blinding light, I could just make out Ethan's form as he ran toward the waiting Orc.

"Ethan, no!" The last thing I wanted was to see any of my princes get hurt. Especially Ethan. He'd already sacrificed so much for me and nearly lost his life once before. I wasn't sure I could handle seeing him barely clinging to life again. I turned, grabbing the shoulders of the female and moving my hands up to what I hoped was her face. "Run, go hide somewhere."

I could feel her nodding in my hands and she pulled away from me. I didn't wait to see where she went before I charged into the light blindly following the sounds of flesh against flesh as Ethan and the Orc engaged in what sounded to be hand-to-hand combat.

*I need to see*, I thought the words, forcing the meaning deep inside as I fought to gain control of the magic chaos I created. I slowed down, extending my fingers in front of me as I waited for the light to fade. Inside, I could now make out the shapes of the two figures. One, much larger than the other.

Not taking the time to consider my actions, I crept around behind the orc, then I jumped on him, wrapping my arms around his thick neck. The creature howled as I dug my fingernails into its shoulders to maintain my position on its sweaty back. A shiver ran through me as I tried not to think too hard about the disgusting beast I had my legs wrapped around.

The light was fading and I could now see in front of me. Momentarily confused, the Orc ignored Ethan, wobbling as it tried to free itself of me. Deciding I was the greater threat, the creature reached behind and swatted at me with his large frying pan sized hands.

I scrambled to the side, trying to avoid getting hit. The first swat missed me, but his other hand grabbed hold of my thigh and tugged. My fingernails bit further into its skin and the orc let out a howl as my nails scratched a line down his back as he pulled my leg free.

I dropped to the ground landing on my back with a thud. For a second, I couldn't breathe as spots danced in my vision. But I regained focus long enough to see Ethan turning the orc's head to the side farther than it should turn until a sickening crack echoed down the empty hallway.

The orc landed on the ground, his lifeless body nearly hitting me on his way down. I scrambled away just in time to avoid having the beast fall on me. Panting, I stared up at Ethan in surprise. I knew he was just as strong and capable as any of the other princes, but I never thought I'd see him kill in such a brutal way.

Without looking back at the fallen Orc, Ethan walked over to me, his brow furrowed in concern. He knelt down in front of me extending a hand toward me. I took it and let him pull me to sitting.

"Are you hurt?" he asked.

I rubbed the back of my head where it had smacked the ground. It was sore, but my vision had cleared and I was able to breathe again. "I think so."

Ethan stroked my cheek. "You are something else, you know that? You stand by helplessly when someone breaks into your room yet the second someone else is in trouble, you act on instinct."

"I couldn't let anything happy to you," I said.

Ethan pressed his forehead to mine. "You won't get rid of me that easily."

Whispered voices filled the hallway and Ethan straightened, turning toward the sound. I looked around.

A couple of doors on the hallway were now cracked open and eyes were peering through to investigate the scene. I didn't realize there would be so many occupied doors in one of Tristan's homes. All the other places we'd been at seemed so vacant.

The white light I had created was completely gone now and I saw the orc lying dead on the ground. Five doors down was Julian, still unmoving.

"Is it over?" a female voice asked from behind me.

I turned around to see the face of the female who seem to be the cause of all of this. "It's over. What happened?"

She looked over at Ethan then lowered her eyes and dropped into a clumsy curtsy while still gripping the bed sheet. "I'm sorry, your grace. I didn't realize we had diplomats in attendance this evening. No one told me. They usually tell us."

I looked over at Ethan, confused. Then, I realized the clothing he was wearing must have identified him to her as one of Tristan's entourage.

The wheels began to spin my head as I put it all together. Hallway full of small, private rooms. A terrified girl, an Orc angry about being kicked out after paying for a full night, an apology for not recognizing a high-ranking guest.

I turned to Ethan. "This is a brothel." I'd never been in a brothel before, but one of the interesting things about being female where I grew up, was that you often went unnoticed in public places. I'd heard enough stories from men over the years to know these kinds of places existed. I just never thought I'd find myself in one.

"You must be new here," the female said to me. "We don't often see males who travel with their own companion."

I glanced from her to Ethan putting her words together. She thought I was his personal courtesan. I shook my head. I had now been referred to as Cormac's lady, Dane's mate, and now Ethan's courtesan.

"She was raised in the Autumn Court," Ethan said. "So she's unused to our ways."

My mouth dropped open and I stared at Ethan in disbelief. "Excuse me?"

"It's alright, Cassia," Ethan said.

His words seemed to confirm the female's suspicions. I had half a mind to yell at him right there and set her straight. But something inside me seemed to be telling me to keep quiet. I could almost believe it was Ethan's voice in my head, urging me for just this once, to keep my mouth shut.

Carefully, I fixed a smile on my face and lowered my eyes, trying to mimic the way the female in front of me behaved around Ethan.

"It's not often that we get girls from other Courts." The girl offered her hand to me. "Would you like me to show you around? I can find you something suitable to wear since your master has left you nothing but a robe." She winked at Ethan, seeming to find it silly.

I looked at Ethan, shocked that he would consider letting me go off with a strange courtesan that neither of us knew. I waited, expecting him to turn her down and decline the invitation for me, but he didn't. "I'm not sure we have time right now."

"Of course we do," Ethan said. "I have some things to work on with the Winter Prince. See that she's back to me in time for supper. I'm staying in the crescent moon suite."

It felt like my entire body went numb as I watched Ethan casually turn away from me and wave nonchalantly as he walked away. Why would Ethan leave me with her? Especially when someone had just tried to kill me?

The girl in front of me tugged on my hand and I looked down, having forgotten that I had taken it. Her green eyes sparkled, clearly thrilled for the distraction or very interested in showing someone new around.

"I'm Lainey. You're Cassia?" she asked as she dragged me down the hallway.

"Yes, Cassia. Nice to meet you, Lainey." I stepped over the fallen arm of the dead orc and carefully kept against the wall to avoid stepping on any other part of him. Lainey didn't seem to even notice or care that there were two dead bodies in the hall-way. "Is this normal here?"

She shrugged. "About once a month or so one of the clients gets a little too rough and the guards take care of them for us." She stopped in front of the door that she'd run from and turned the handle, opening it.

She let go of my hand and swept her arm toward the room. "It's part of why girls find their way here, even from other courts. It's the only house of its kind. The only place we're treated with respect and we have a choice in our clients and the right to tell them no. If the client doesn't listen, he or she faces the consequences."

I thought back to the type of men that I'd heard discussing their visits to brothels. I couldn't imagine any of them being someone's choice; I also couldn't imagine an orc being someone's choice. "An orc?"

"I shouldn't have agreed. My intuition was telling me there was something off about him." She shook her head. "But we charge so much more for non Fae guests. I send my money back home to my family, and they needed a little extra this month, so I agreed. I'm sure you know how it is. Though, I must say, you got very lucky. Most girls would kill to be the personal consort of a Fae as attractive as yours."

She settled onto a pile of cushions in one corner of the floor and patted a space next to her on the ground. I followed her, my bare feet sinking into the plush carpet of the room.

As I walked over I glanced around the small, private room. It had a large bed that took up most of the space, which was probably why she had cushions on the floor and against the wall. It was her only non-bed seating. Up against the opposite wall was a small dressing table with a stool tucked below the cluttered surface. I could see brushes and powders and various other forms of makeup scattered across the top.

On the remaining free wall was a curtain that was half drawn. Beyond the opening, I could see gowns and lacy clothes. The room was small, but every inch of it screamed luxury.

Lainey stood. "It's freezing today isn't it?" She walked over to the curtain acting as a cover to her closet. "Some days I don't even bother with clothes. It just makes it so much more inconvenient to take them off later, you know what I mean?" She pushed the curtain to the side. "What does your master prefer? Formal? Informal? Kinky?"

I blinked a few times, trying to let her words sink in. "Usually I just wear trousers and a tunic."

"Peasant girl? I wouldn't have guessed he was the type. But they all have their things, don't they? I've learned that often, the more well off they seem on the outside, the dirtier they are in the inside." She handed me a simple blue dress. "I don't usually wear trousers, this is the closest I've got."

Grateful, I took the dress from her. "Thank you." I turned, glancing around for any place I could get a moment's privacy to change. The room was completely exposed, there was nowhere you could walk to, to dress without someone else seeing you.

"How's your male? Does he treat you as well in the bedroom as he did today? I mean, he must like you an awful lot to be willing to kill for you."

I turned back to Lainey, still clutching the dress in my hands. How did I explain how I felt about Ethan to a stranger? "We've been through a lot together."

"You're very lucky, you know that?" she asked.

"I know," I said.

Lainey dropped the sheet she'd been holding and started to dig through her closet. Startled, I looked down at my feet to give her some privacy. All the princes had told me that things were different in Faerie, that sex wasn't demonized the way it was in the human realm. I glanced back up at Lainey. She didn't seem to mind that she was naked in front of a total stranger.

It seemed, that even when it came to someone they were not going to tumble in bed with, the Fae were not shy about their bodies. At least Lainey wasn't. And she had no reason to be. Her skin was smooth and flawless. And like the male Fae princes it had that same slightly iridescent sheen to it. She was about my height, with a similar slender build, though her hips and breasts had a bit more of a curve to them than mine ever had.

Lainey stopped digging through the closet and turned to glance at me. "Like what you see? It's all right, lots of the girls here like both males and females. Sometimes, you just need to be with someone who's soft and sweet and understands where we like to be touched." She winked at me then turned her attention back to the closet and selected a dress.

Face heating, I turned away from her. I was sure getting an education in the ways of Fae sexuality today. Hesitantly, I dropped the robe I had been clinging to and slipped the blue dress over my head as quickly as possible.

When I turned back around, Lainey was watching me. "I can see why he chose you. You're just as beautiful as he is."

"Thank you," I said, "And thank you for the dress."

She smiled, then walked back over to the cushions and plopped down on the floor. I joined her, settling in nearby.

"Sometimes I think it would be nice to find a male to keep me as his personal courtesan, but I do enjoy meeting new guests. I worry I'd get bored if I stayed with one. Does he ever share you?" she asked.

My mind flashed back to my tumble with Dane this morning. "I guess so."

"That's kind of him. I imagine it makes it more fun," she said. "I have a few regulars, but sometimes you need a change, you know?"

"What about love?" I asked. "Don't you ever wonder about it?"

"You mean mating?" She shrugged. "I heard a story once, of a working girl at a place like this who grew so close to one of her clients, she thought it might be a mating bond. So she went to visit him in town only to discover he was already married. He agreed it was likely they shared the bond, but he wasn't interested in having more than one wife. She was so heartbroken that she jumped into the lake and never swam back to shore."

"That's a terrible story," I said.

"I know," Lainey said. "Some of the girls here didn't have the resources, you know?"

I nodded, feeling like I was starting to understand Lainey and the other girls who worked here. "How long have you been here?"

"Here in the House of the Moon? Or here in the business?" she asked, lifting an eyebrow.

"Both," I said.

"Seven years at the House of the Moon, twenty-two years in the business," she smiled, "I figure five or ten more and I can retire. Maybe I'll find that mate. You never know."

Immortality really changed things. Where I came from, the girls who worked in the pleasure houses often didn't live long enough to see life outside them. I wondered if given the opportunity, if I'd have chosen a life like this over being married to the Baron. The thought never crossed my mind. I wasn't sure I was strong enough to ever do what Lainey did.

A dragging sound from outside the door made me turn away from Lainey. Instantly on alert I jumped to my feet ready to run or fight if someone was trying to attack again.

"Sounds like the guards are here to move the bodies," Lainey said. "You're safe."

I watched the door for a few more seconds to make sure it didn't open. Once I was satisfied the sounds in the hallway were staying in the hallway, I sat back down.

"Why are there royal guards here? Why do they seem to work for Tristan?" I asked.

Lainey's eyebrows rose and she stared at me as if in disbelief. "Tristan? Do you mean the Prince? I've never heard anyone use his first name before. So is that who you really belong to? Are you sneaking off with one of his men? Oh, Cassia, that's dangerous. Please tell me you're not going behind his back."

"No, no. I don't belong to Prince Tristan, I mean, His Grace. I don't belong to anybody," I said.

"Of course not, neither do I," she said. "But you have a master, same as me. And I get it if you don't want to admit it, but please, be smart."

"I'm not his," I said. "He's helping me with something."

Lainey narrowed her eyes. "The Winter Prince isn't the helping type. Be careful with him. I've heard enough stories to know he's not someone you want to cross."

"Like what?" I asked.

She shook her head. "I can't. It's not allowed."

"I understand." I didn't want her to get in trouble, so I didn't press. But I had to admit, I wanted to know more about the things she knew.

"But to answer your question, the Royal Guard is stationed here because this used to be one of the grand palaces of the Winter Court. The King converted it into his own personal brothel a few hundred years ago, and stationed his own personal guards to keep all of his women safe. Eventually, he let some of his friends visit from time to time and it became a place for dignitaries and high rollers from all over Faerie.

"The place developed a reputation and eventually the King lost interest, but the high-end clientele continued to come. After the war, I suppose they had to get less picky with who they took as clients since they couldn't open it up to all the Courts. It must've been glorious in its heyday, only the most elite Fae from every Court. They come here from far and wide just to spend an evening with one of the girls at the House of the Moon. Now, we still have protection from the Royal Guard, but we'll take almost anyone who can pay and has a decent reputation. Clearly, someone made a mistake letting in that Orc."

"What about the Winter Prince? Does he visit often?" I held my breath as I waited for her answer, unsure if she'd consider this too risky to discuss.

She leaned in, moving her face closer to mine. Her green eyes seemed to be looking internally, trying to read me. I fought the urge to blink and stared back at her not wanting to give anything away. She leaned back, a hint of a smirk playing on her lips. "No.

You don't need to be jealous. He hasn't visited since his wife died."

"Do you think he loved her?" I asked.

"It was an arranged marriage, but I think they were meant to be. I hate that the other girls talk about her sometimes. She visited with him, apparently they shared everything. But none of the other participants fully felt like they were included in activities. They said they could hardly ever get in between the two of them because despite the large group, he only had eyes for her. As far as a brothel love story goes, it's probably one of the most romantic ones I've ever heard."

"He still doesn't seem like he's over her," I said without really thinking.

"Have you told him how you feel?" she asked. "I mean, at first I thought you might belong to him and that maybe you were sneaking around behind his back. But now, I think you belong to the one I met in the hall, but you don't want to."

I turned and looked at her and tried to mask my shocked expression with a laugh. "I don't have feelings for him. That's ridiculous. I never could. And I'm perfectly happy with Ethan."

"Of course you are. Of course you don't have feelings for anyone else," Lainey said. "Don't worry, I won't tell your master." She reached out and grabbed my hands closing hers around mine. "You might not be one of the girls who works here, but you're one of us. We're a sisterhood. What we say privately to each other, never reaches any others' ears but our own."

"I'm not exactly the same," I said. Ethan seemed to want me to pretend I was his courtesan, but Lainey was so sweet and so open that I felt bad lying to her.

"That's not important. Titles aren't important between us. What is important is how we treat each other and how we stand together when we know one of us is in pain. I don't know you, I can tell you've been through a lot. And I can tell you still have a long way to go before you feel at peace."

Laney's words rang of truth and they stung to hear. She was right, I had a long way to go, even if I had no idea what was ahead of me. I squeezed her hands back. "Thank you. Hopefully one day I can return the favor."

Dropping my hands, Lainey stood. "No need. Sometimes we meet the right Fae at the right time. I'm glad if I could be of some help. Now let's get you back before supper. We wouldn't want your master to think I stole you away."

# Chapter Twelve

❦

This time, when I walked down the hall and past the blood stains on the ground, I heard whispers and giggles behind the closed doors. I wondered how many girls worked and lived there and how man clients they each saw. Lainey's life seemed so interesting and terrifying at the same time.

She led me down a set of stairs and down another hall lined with closed doors. None of the doors in either hall had been marked but I saw an occasional note or scroll stuck in the seam, waiting for someone to open the door and find the message.

At the end of the second hall, we reached another stairwell. This one was dark and the walls were black rock. We were heading into a basement. "Down here, really?"

She nodded. "The suites for dignitaries were added later. Most of our visitors stay with one of the girls when they stay the night. But over the years, I guess there were enough long term stays to warrant the addition of some private suites. They're nice. I've done a few private parties in them for some of the high rollers."

I wondered if that was what Tristan and his wife did when they came here. A flash of skin on skin passed before my vision and even though the moment was over nearly as quick as it arrived, I knew it had been of Tristan with me. The scent of him lingered around me as if he'd been standing right next to me. A shudder through my core went right down between my legs and I clenched my thighs against the unexpected arousal. I needed to stop thinking about Tristan like that.

By the time we stopped in front of a black door with a painting of a crescent moon on the front of it, the sensitive area between my legs was tingling. It seemed all this discussion of sex had woken the part of me that longed to be touched and no amount of inner chiding was sending the sensation away.

"You know, we're always looking for new girls of quality," Lainey said, fist floating above the door, ready to knock. "Just in case you ever want a change of scenery. I'm sure a recommendation from His Grace would be enough to get you one of the best rooms in the house."

"Thank you, that's exceptionally sweet," I said.

"I get it," Lainey said. "I don't think I could walk away from an exclusive contract, either. Even if I was in love with someone else."

"I'm not," I said, denying her words again. "I might even be in love with Ethan for all I know."

Of course, that was when the door opened. Ethan stared at me, one eyebrow raised. Lainey stood frozen, her fist still hanging in midair. She dropped her hand and curtseyed while stifling a giggle.

I felt my face heat and I knew I was bright red. There was nothing I would be able to say or do to get out of this one.

Lainey leaned closer to me and pressed her lips against my ear. "Sounds like things are complicated. If you need a friend, you know where to find me."

"Thank you," I said, quietly.

She took a step away from me and inclined her head before turning to walk away, leaving me alone with Ethan.

"So," Ethan said, moving to the side so I could enter

the room.

I took a deep breath, still feeling the burn of my cheeks, and walked into the room.

Ethan closed the door behind us and walked over to where I was standing in the center of the large suite. Lainey was right, I had my doubts that a basement room would impress, but this was a room fit for royalty. And I knew because I'd spent the last several days staying with four princes. A roaring fire burned in the corner, a large rug spread in front of it. Two couches faced each other on either side of the rug with little end tables on each end. A high four-poster bed was on the wall opposite the fireplace and unlike Lainey's room, there was plenty of extra space to walk around or fit extra people.

Ethan waited quietly nearby, his hands clasped in front of him. Being the gentleman that he was, he seemed to be waiting for me to decide if I wanted to acknowledge what I'd said. I considered ignoring the words, but I knew they were out there. "Ethan, I..."

He moved closer to me, his expression sympathetic, but he didn't touch me.

Swallowing hard, I looked down at my feet, then back up at him. "Ethan, I think I might be falling for you. But..."

He waited patiently, silently urging me to continue.

"It's not just you," I finished.

"I know," he said, closing the gap between us.

He was close enough now that if I leaned in just a little, I'd be touching him. My body responded to his closeness, my thighs aching to wrap themselves around him. I needed him the way I needed to breathe.

As if he could feel my yearning, he slid his fingers through my hair, stopping when his large hand was cradling the back of my head. When I didn't resist, he gently urged me closer. I moved with him, my lips felt like they were swelling in anticipation of the kiss.

When he pressed his lips to mine, I felt a wave of calm rush though me as the heat rose between my thighs. I'd lost my under-garments after I'd left the scene of the attack and now wetness began to slide down my thigh as Ethan wrapped his other arm around me, pulling my body against his. I could feel the bulge of his erection pressing into my thigh, making my breathing even more shallow than it already was. I wanted him. I needed him.

He kissed me hungrily, more forcefully than he had last time we were together. It was as if he needed me just as much as I needed him. His hands dropped to my hips and I felt him bunching up my dress as he slipped his tongue into my mouth. My tongue met his in a playful flicker before I bit down on his lower lip. He moaned into my mouth then broke away from the kiss.

With a growl, Ethan lifted the dress over my head. Then, he pulled his tunic off and stripped his trousers off faster than I thought possible. I stared at him for a moment, my breathing heavy as I drank in every inch of his bare skin. His sculpted chest moved up and down as he breathed, but I dropped my eyes lower, not lingering there. Past his rippling stomach, past the cut V of his hips, down to where his erection was already alert and ready for me.

My skin felt like it was on fire. I wanted to jump on him, throw him on the bed, keep him pinned down until I made him groan in ecstasy. But something told me that wasn't the way he wanted to bed me. I waited to see what Ethan had in mind. He wasn't as intense as Dane. He was gentle and sweet our first time—my first time.

Ethan moved toward me slowly. Each step he took seemed to make my heart beat faster in anticipation. Finally, he was directly in front of me again and I leaned in to him, eager to feel his touch.

He dragged his fingertips up my arm, sending a trail of goose-bumps in their wake. His touch made my legs tremble. When his fingers reached my neck, he slid his hand around the back of my head and guided me to him. My breasts pressed into his chest, his erection pressed into my thigh. I thought he was going to kiss me again, but he turned my head and instead of placing his lips on mine, he gently traced his tongue along my ear. I shivered, letting out a moan.

With a playful smile on his lips, he pulled away from me then took my hand in his. Silently, he led me to the bed. Like the gentleman he was, he pulled the covers down for us and guided me down into the center of the soft bed.

He was on top of me now, staring into my eyes with a hungry expression that would have looked at home on a wild animal. He grinned, showing his sharp canines. "What is it about you, Cassia?"

I reached for his face and stroked his cheek. "What is it about you?"

He buried his face in my neck, kissing and sucking on the sensitive skin. I moaned again, surprised by how much his touch sent waves of pleasure through me. I wasn't going to be able to hold off much longer. The wetness between my thighs grew with each nip of his teeth against my skin. The whole lower part of my body ached for relief. "Please," I whispered.

Ethan didn't hesitate. Knowing exactly what I wanted, he slid inside me in one fluid stroke. We both gasped in unison, satisfied relief coupled with pure bliss as he thrust inside me.

He pulled me closer, our bodies working together in a perfect rhythm. Ethan's movements were tender, his touches gentle. And with each passing second, I felt my attachment to him grow. How could I doubt my feelings for him? We had a connection I couldn't deny.

Ethan pressed his lips to mine and wrapped his arms around me, rolling me on top of him. When he was on his back, he broke free of the kiss. I sat above him, looking down at his beautiful face. "I think I'm in love with you."

He took my hands, our fingers interlaced together. "I love you, too."

# Chapter Thirteen

※❦※

As I laid in Ethan's arms listening to his breathing, I let my mind replay the events of the evening. Someone had broken into the room I was alone in. While I had no proof the assassin was there for me, it sure seemed like too much of a coincidence to not be connected to me. Then, there was the Orc going crazy and threatening Lainey. I never did ask her what it was she refused to do. I wondered what a courtesan would say no to when it came to an Orc client. I liked Lainey, though, and it seemed inappropriate to ask. Not that it mattered anymore anyway, the Orc was dead. At Ethan's hands. Which was something I never expected to see.

I looked over at the sleeping Spring Prince. He looked so peaceful while he slept. Like a work of art; perfectly sculpted and proportioned. I tried to settle into his arms while telling myself that I shouldn't worry about things I couldn't control. But that wasn't possible. I needed to know what was happening.

Quietly, I lifted Ethan's arm from my waist and shimmied off the bed to avoid disturbing him. On the floor, I found the borrowed blue dress and pulled it over my head. I was sure my blonde curls were a mess, but there wasn't much I could do about that right then. So I tied them in a knot in the back of my head as best I could. Then, I tiptoed to the door and glanced back at Ethan. His breathing was still steady and even. Holding my breath, I turned the doorknob, hoping it wouldn't make too much noise. The door was well oiled and opened without a sound. I wondered if that was typical maintenance in a brothel. Having discretion was probably a major selling point.

I crept down the stone hall, the cold floor seeping into my bare feet. Wishing I had thought to grab my boots before I left the upper room where I'd stripped for the bath, I wiggled my toes to keep the blood flowing and contained. I wasn't exactly sure where I was going or what I was looking for. All I knew was that something didn't feel right. I wanted answers. Especially about the Fae female who climbed into a brothel.

At first, I thought I had to be the target, but the more I thought about it, the more I started to wonder if her knife had been meant for a visiting dignitary. Who usually used the room they'd placed me in? Was it empty and that's why it was chosen? Or was there a specific person she was targeting. If that was the case, was it meant to be me or someone else? If it was me, how did she know I was there?

Voices sounded from behind one of the closed doors in the dark hallway. Each of the doors had a celestial symbol on them and from what I could tell, the sound was coming from the room with a full moon on the door.

I crept toward the door and pressed my ear against the painted wood. Two male voices carried through the door. They were muffled and difficult to make out. None of the words were clear but after a minute or two of listening, I was almost sure it was Cormac and Tristan. Why were the two of them in the room together? Was Dane in there with them?

Something slammed on the other side of the door and one of the voices raised to a yell. Whatever the wood was made out of, it prevented me from hearing the details, but I could tell there was an argument going on. My heart raced and I wondered if I should intervene. From what I'd seen of the two of them, they should never be alone together. They could very nearly kill one another. Another slam. Another round of yelling.

Silencing the little voice in my head that told me it was a bad idea, I turned the handle and opened the door.

Inside the room, there were two Fae males staring at me that I didn't recognize. I was so sure it was Tristan and Cormac's voices I'd heard. How had I been so wrong? "Sorry," I mumbled, tugging the door closed behind me.

One of the males crossed the room in a heartbeat and set his hand on top of mine. "Please, stay a while. We were just discussing you."

The hair on the back of my neck stood and I knew I was in danger. This had been a very bad idea. Why hadn't I listened to the little voice? My jaw tensed as I realized it was that hunter intuition I'd laughed about. I should have listened better to Cormac. "No, thank you. I must be going. I'm expected."

"No you're not," the second Fae said. "They're all asleep. It's just us. Come on in for chat."

I pulled my hand away and turned to run, but someone grabbed hold of my arm and yanked me into the room. I heard the door slam behind me as one of the males pushed me into a chair.

He was tall and scruffy looking. With wild brown hair and bushy eyebrows. I wouldn't have even guessed he was Fae if not for the pointed ears. He was stockier in his build than the princes, shorter, and thicker, but he looked strong. "We need to know everything you have planned for Queen's Trial. You leave anything out, we'll kill you."

I sat on the chair, grabbing the edges of the seat, trying to figure out what was happening. Despite the haggard appearance of the one Fae, both males wore expensive looking clothing. I was grateful they were wearing clothing at all after the Orc situation. "Who are you?"

One of the males slapped me across the face. I gasped and pressed my open palm against the stinging on my cheek.

"Answer the question," he growled.

I narrowed my eyes at my assailant. He was tall, with long dark hair and nearly black eyes. His nose was crooked, as if it had been broken and healed incorrectly. I wanted to memorize his face because I knew my princes would ask me for every detail. "I can't answer your question."

He lifted his hand and I flinched. He held it above me. "Answer."

"I don't have any plans for Queen's Trial so you can hit me all you want, but you're not going to get any answers from me."

The dark haired male hesitated, as if unsure of how to respond to me. Then, just when I thought I might have reasoned with him, he slapped me again.

This time, I tasted blood at the corner of my mouth and I reached up to check on the wound. Sure enough, when I pulled my hand away from my lips, crimson blood coated my fingertips. "You're going to regret that."

"Your escorts aren't here to save you now," the scruffy one said.

"I just watched one of those escorts you mention break the neck of an orc with his bare hands." I let the words sink in for a moment. "I can't imagine what they'll do to you when they find out you hurt me."

"We're not trying to hurt you," the dark haired Fae said.

I gently touched my sore cheek in response.

"Look, we know you're going to be a contender at the Trials, we need to know what you are planning," he said.

I narrowed my eyes. "You sent the assassin, didn't you? All of this is about some stupid competition."

"Assassin?" the scruffy one scratched his head.

Just then, the door flew open, sending shards of wood flying. I covered my face and turned away from the flying debris. When I looked back at the doorway, I saw Ethan, Cormac, Dane, and Tristan staring back at me.

I didn't wait for instructions. Seizing my opportunity, I bolted from the chair and ran to the door, dashing between Dane and Tristan until I was standing behind all four of my princes.

"Your Grace," scruffy said, getting on his knees. "We didn't realize she was your champion."

Cormac took a step toward the cowering male. "Dwane. I should have known. How did you even gain entry into the Winter Court?"

Dwane still had his head down. "My mother was Winter, father Autumn."

"So he's yours to punish, Cormac," Tristan said. "Unless you'd like me to assume the responsibility."

"He committed acts of violence against another Fae in your court, Tristan. He's yours if the punishment is severe enough."

I was surprised to hear the venom in Cormac's voice. What were they going to do to these two?

Tristan stepped forward, leaving me standing right behind Dane. I moved closer to him until my shoulder was touching him.

"For attempted murder?" Tristan asked. "The punishment is death."

"We weren't going to murder anyone," Dwane said. "Honest, we just wanted to hear her strategy. Your Grace, our family has been struggling ever since the war and this year, we have our Isla. She has a chance to win the Trials. We wanted to give her every advantage. It's no different than what any other house is doing right now. Even your girl was illegally raised in the human world."

"What was that?" Cormac said.

"I didn't mean any disrespect, Your Grace," Dwane said. "You have every right to hide her in the human realm. It's not my business."

"You certainly made it your business when you trapped her in here," Ethan said, stepping forward to join Cormac and Tristan.

"They didn't send the assassin," Tristan said, turning to Cormac. "They aren't skilled enough to even know that Cassia's not in the Trials."

"She's not?" Dwane said. "But everyone has been saying she's the one to beat."

"Who says this?" Cormac said.

"It's all over the Autumn Court. The fact that you and the other two princes were championing a single entry instead of one per house," Dwane said.

"Now we know why someone tried to kill you," Dane said quietly.

"Guards," Tristan called. "Take them away."

Dane grabbed me and moved me away from the doorway just as four guards walked into the room. They must have been waiting just outside the door for Tristan's orders.

Dwane and his friend were silent, heads hanging in defeat as they were escorted from the room. I had never felt like my life was in danger while I was in the room, but I wasn't sorry to see them go.

"Does this mean I have to worry about monsters and Fae trying to kill me now?" I asked.

"We're not going to let anyone or anything kill you, Cassia," Cormac said. Then he turned to Ethan. "Keep her with you tonight. The rest of us are going to follow up on that lead."

"What lead?" I asked.

"We'll talk about it in the morning," Cormac said.

My shoulders sank. Back to the secrets with Cormac.

He walked out of the room followed by Dane and Tristan. My heart ached as I watched them all leave. Especially since Tristan never even acknowledged me once.

Ethan's warm hand took a hold of mine. "You weren't in the room so I summoned the others."

"Thank you," I said. "Am I ever going to get to know what's going on here?"

"You will," he said. "Give them more time. I don't think they want to tell you until they know the truth."

"Do you know what they found?" I asked, then frowned. It was clear from Ethan's expression he was in the loop. "Of course you do."

Ethan sighed. "Please, Cassia. Just this once, let someone else take care of you for a change."

# Chapter Fourteen

There were worse places to be than snuggled in Ethan's arms. Far worse. His warm, firm chest pressed against my side as his arm that was embracing me rose and fell with my breathing. I adjusted, burrowing as close to him as I could. Even though I felt safe with Ethan, it was difficult to sleep knowing that there were Fae out there looking for me. Why did they all think I was part of the Queen's Trial nonsense? I had no interest in competing for a title. I didn't like the rules and pretentious nature of the court. I was sure the Fae Court wasn't much different than the human Royal Court. All I wanted was to get some help figuring this magic out and start finding out where I fit in to this place. I wanted a home and the ability to take care of myself. And if I was being honest with myself, I wanted my princes. All of them. Maybe even Tristan.

The problem was I wasn't sure I was good for them. I knew how Ethan felt about me and I knew how I felt about him, but there were people trying to kill me and monsters breaking free of the Under for me. Was I bringing them down with me? What if someone tried to break in again? What if they hurt Ethan instead of me?

Ethan kissed the top of my head and I turned to look at him. In the dim light of the dying fire, I could see his green eyes staring down at me. "You need to rest."

"How can I?" I asked. "I don't want anything to happen to you."

Ethan chuckled softly. "Oh, Cassia." He pulled me tighter. "How do you think I feel about you?"

"It's not you they're after, though," I said. "I'm risking all of you by staying with you."

"Cassia," Ethan said. "How do you think I knew you were in trouble tonight when the Orc threatened you? Or when you went missing from the bed?"

"You told me you could sense where I was," I said.

"It's so much more than that now, Cassia."

"What do you mean?" I asked.

"I knew you were in danger. I could feel it as if you were calling to me," he said.

My heart pounded against my ribs and my memories spun back to the night at the wedding. When Ethan had told me about how Fae mate. "Are you saying?" I couldn't finish the thought. My chest tightened and I held my breath, afraid to hope that he felt as strongly about me as I did about him. Even if I thought he'd be safer without me, I couldn't imagine being away from him.

"I told you I love you, Cassia. But it's so much deeper than that," he slid a stray curl away from my face, "tell me you feel it too."

"I do," I said. "I feel it."

"So you know I'm not going anywhere. And you know I'm going to keep you safe, no matter what." He kissed my forehead again. "Now go to sleep."

My whole body felt warm as a relieved satisfaction settled around me. What Ethan and I had was simple and pure. I knew I could count on him the same way he could count on me. I'd never felt as comfortable or safe as I did in his arms. Finally, I settled into a dreamless sleep.

When I woke the next morning, Ethan was already awake, sitting in a chair near the large fireplace. I tossed the blankets aside and stepped onto the freezing stone floor.

He looked up at me as I padded over to him. "Good morning."

The only light in the room came from the healthy fire crackling away in the hearth. "What time is it?"

"After breakfast," he said.

I sat down on the arm of the chair. "How long have you been awake?"

"Not long," he said.

After everything that had happened last night, I wasn't sure where to begin this morning. I sat quietly next to Ethan, enjoying the warmth from the fire and his closeness to me. "It's quiet here."

"Most of the people who visit here sleep late," he said.

"That makes sense." My stomach growled and my cheeks heated in embarrassment. "Sorry."

Ethan smiled. "I'm sure we can find something in the kitchens. Plus, Cormac is probably waiting for us."

Part of me didn't want to leave the little sanctuary of the basement room. There were no windows and only one way in - through a locked door. Once we left, I was exposed. "That lead, from last night, you think they figured anything out?"

"Don't worry," he said. "If they haven't yet, they will soon."

Quickly, I pulled on the dress Lainey lent me. Then, I followed Ethan out of the door into the dark basement hallway. The stone floor was cold under my feet and I hoped I'd be able to hunt down a pair of boots soon. As we walked toward the stairs, I had the odd sense that Ethan and I were alone. The hallway was silent but it didn't feel like the type of quiet that came from sleeping. It was more than that. Suddenly, I was happy we were leaving the dark basement behind. There was a stifled feeling down there and it didn't sit well with me.

The light on the main floor was bright when we emerged from the basement stairwell. Weak sunlight poured in through the windows, but there was no warmth from the light. Everything about the heart of the Winter Court was cold.

I expected to see servants or other Fae, but just as the basement had been, it felt abandoned. "Where is everyone?"

Ethan walked ahead of me, peeking into the sitting room and the kitchen.

"We're up here," Dane's voice came from behind me.

I turned to see him on the stairway, walking down to us.

"I had a feeling you were up," he said, stopping in front of me. He kissed my cheek. "Were you able to get any rest?" His question was laced with genuine concern.

"I did, thank you."

"We're upstairs," Dane said to Ethan. "Fourth floor. We have news."

"What is it?" I asked. "What did you find out?"

"I can't possibly tell you," Dane said. "It would ruin all of Cormac's fun."

We walked into a large, nearly empty room at the top of the stairs. In the center of the room was a massive table littered with small objects and rolled up parchment. A wood stove in the corner heated the room so it was warmer than the basement had been despite an entire wall of glass windows that looked out over the city.

Cormac was standing next to the window, staring out at the street below.

He turned at the sound of us walking into the room. "I wondered when you'd join us."

"You could have woken me," I said. "I thought we were in a hurry to get to the Queen's palace."

"There are some complications," Cormac said.

"Complications?" I asked, peering around him to get a view of the window. "What were you looking at?"

"Guards," Cormac said, gesturing behind him.

I padded over to the large glass pained window and looked down. We were in one of the taller buildings in the bustling city. In the street below, I saw people walking back and forth along with carts and horses. Everyone seemed to be fighting for the ability to move through the crowded street. Part of the congestion was the fact that there was a large group of guards blocking half of the street directly in front of the building we were in. "Is that really necessary?"

"Why?" I asked.

"Because you've drawn a lot of attention to yourself," Tristan's voice carried into the room from behind me.

I turned away from the window and bit down the comment I wanted to make about him finally speaking to me again. "Is this all about Queen's Trial?"

"It started off that way," Tristan said. "But now, it's about your Queen."

My brow furrowed. "I don't understand."

"You've created quite the sensation. A highborn Fae nobody ever heard of before who has been placed under the protection of the Autumn Prince. You ride with a prince of each of the four courts. It's made a lot of people nervous, including my own nobles," Tristan said.

"Is that why I was attacked?" I asked. "But I thought that was someone from the Summer Court."

"The first assassin was from the Summer Court, the males who questioned you last night were from the Autumn Court."

"How did they even get in?" I asked. "I thought they needed Winter Fae blood."

"We're still working on that part," Tristan said, his jaw tightening.

I looked at Cormac, hoping he'd clarify some of this for me. "What now?"

"Now, we wait," he said. "For the Queen's sister."

"Wait?" I asked, my stomach churning with unease.

"She's on her way here," Dane said. "News of you reached the Queen and she's requested we meet with her sister before we travel to her palace."

"Alright," I said. "I suppose that's good, right? We let her know what's going on and she helps relay our message. But that doesn't explain everything else. What about the nobles who called in their soldiers?"

Tristan raised an eyebrow. "You know about that?"

My eyes widened and I looked to Cormac, wondering if I'd said something wrong. He'd trusted me with that information.

"We talked about it," Cormac said. "Tristan is aware of the issue. It has nothing to do with you."

"But that sounds bad," I said.

"Don't worry about that," Tristan said.

A gentle knock on the open door caused all of us to turn to see the newcomer. Lainey and another female were standing at the door. They both curtseyed low, avoiding eye contact with Tristan. "Your Grace, we were told you wanted to see us."

"Yes, thank you for coming," he said. "I require assistance with my lady friend. She needs to be properly attired for a visit with an especially important diplomat."

Tristan walked over to them, a smirk on his lips. He stopped right in front of them and cocked his head to the side. "They tell me you two are the most experienced ladies in the house. They tell me you're the best. And the most discreet."

My chest felt like it was on fire as I watched him shamelessly flirting with the two courtesans in front of me. Seeing him turn on the charm for other females was nearly painful to witness. I clenched my teeth and felt my nostrils flare as I tried to calm my temper. It didn't make sense for me to care about how he acted or who he was with, but the jealousy surged through me the same way it would if it had been Ethan standing there flirting with them.

Tristan touched Lainey's cheek. "You'll be compensated well for your efforts." Tristan leaned closer to her and whispered something I couldn't hear.

Lainey giggled, and lowered her eyes again, playing the chaste maiden. My cheeks heated as I watched her, knowing there was nothing chaste about her. Was he making plans with her? Without thinking I took a few steps closer to them.

Tristan looked up as I approached. His eyes flashed with mischief as he stood back up to his full height. "Don't worry, princess. They'll take good care of you."

I knew my face was turning an even darker shade of red. "I'm not a princess."

"Cassia, just go with them," Cormac said.

I sighed and ignored the grin on Tristan's face as I walked forward, making sure I bumped into him as I passed.

# Chapter Fifteen

Lainey and the other female were silent as we walked down the stairs. We reached Lainey's floor and I continued to follow the silent courtesans. I grimaced at the blood stain on the carpet and forced myself to keep my eyes up, away from the place the Orc and the guard had died just last night. I paused in front of Lainey's door, expecting her to stop, but she continued on to the end of the hall.

Finally, she opened the last door in the hallway and inclined her head in a subtle bow. I narrowed my eyes at her, hoping for an explanation but she kept her eyes averted. "In here?"

She nodded.

Feeling cut off and alone, I walked into the room and stopped right inside the door. The floor was a cool, shiny stone and the room was lined with rows and rows of clothing along each wall. In the center of the room stood a large bathtub. Steam rose from the water already waiting in the tub and my shoulders involuntarily relaxed as the promise of a relaxing bath loomed in front of me.

I heard the click of the door as it closed and spun around to face Lainey and the other female. Lainey did a quick glance around the room, then her stoic expression gave way to a smile. "I would have kept your secret last night. You didn't have to pretend you were a courtesan."

"I'm so sorry," I said.

"Are you really a princess?" the other female asked. She had long, straight black hair that hung to her mid-back. She was about a head shorter than me. Her features were delicate but her eyes were larger than most Fae I saw.

I shook my head. "No, Tristan knew it would bother me if he called me that."

The new female gasped, then giggled as she turned to Lainey. "You were right. She does use his name."

I covered my face with my hands, feeling embarrassed for slipping again. The last thing I wanted was for word to get back to Tristan, the Winter Prince, that I was disrespecting him. He was helping me and I didn't want to be rude.

"Don't worry," Lainey said. "Like I said last night, your words are safe with us. You might not be working, but I have a feeling you understand. Besides, we were told we're getting a Lady ready for an important event."

"You might not be a princess," the new female said, "but you're clearly high ranking."

"Maybe," I said, not really thinking about how the word would sound.

"That's enough, Jae. She doesn't have to tell us. It's clearly complicated," Lainey said.

"It is," I agreed. I'd spent last night with Ethan. The handsome Spring Prince that I felt a mating bond with. But the night before, I'd been with Dane. And my feelings for him were intense and hot and confusing. Then there was Cormac and our almost kiss. At least it felt like that. And I wanted him to kiss me. I wanted him to do all sorts of things to me.

"Well, if I had a chance to have a night with His Grace, I certainly wouldn't turn it down," Jae said, winking at me.

My cheeks heated. Tristan. His Grace. The Winter Prince. He

was speaking to me again, at least. A vision burst into view of my legs wrapped around Tristan's waist. Neither of us were clothed. My thighs clenched and I squeezed my eyes closed to try to clear the picture in my mind. I turned down his offer to sleep in the princess suite, then I'd slapped him in the face. "I'm pretty sure there's no chance of that for me."

"He is a prince," Jae said. "I'm sure his man would share if he wanted you."

The thought of Tristan's mouth exploring my body sent tingles to the place between my legs. "I don't want to talk about this anymore."

"Jae, leave her alone." Lainey turned to me. "You'll have to forgive her, My Lady."

"You don't have to call me that," I said. "Cassia is fine."

Lainey nodded. "Alright, Cassia. Let's get you ready for that visitor."

I wasn't used to bathing in front of strangers, but neither of the females showed any sign of giving me privacy. Though, based on what happened last time I'd taken a bath, I should be grateful for their company.

"So, are you going to tell us why someone from the Summer Court tried to kill you? You didn't share that with me earlier," Lainey said.

"How did you know about that?" I stepped into the rose scented water and used my fingers to send the floating petals swirling around me. "Nothing stays secret here, does it?"

Lainey poured warm water on the back of my head, soaking my hair. I leaned back so it wouldn't run into my eyes as she worked the tangles out with her fingers.

"You are correct. The interesting thing about the House of the Moon, is that nobody considers us important enough to censor themselves around us. We probably have more knowledge of the inner workings of the Winter Court that anyone save the Prince himself," Lainey said.

My ears perked at her comment. I had a feeling conversations were very free around these females. "Yes, I was attacked by someone. Why do I have a feeling that you know more than me?"

"She calls His Grace by his first name, but he won't tell you what he knows about your assassin?" The other girl asked.

"She's a lady," Lainey said. "I'm sure he's trying to protect her."

The other girl, Jae, rolled her eyes and handed me a bar of pink soap in the shape of a rose. Apparently, the theme of this bath was to get me smelling as much like a flower as possible. I took the soap from her, then worked it into a lather between my hands, grateful that they were allowing me to soap myself up. Lainey had moved on to a brush, working the tangles out of my hair slowly.

"I sort of did something to upset him," I said. "I think he's withholding information from me now as punishment."

"So does that mean it's over between the two of you?" Lainey asked.

"I told you there's nothing between us," I said.

Lainey stopped brushing my hair. "You share with us, we'll share with you."

"What happened to not talking about him?" I asked.

"I won't share stories that aren't mine to share. It sounds like you have reliable information, I can't get punished for that," she said.

"No way," my cheeks heated. It was bad enough that I had accused Tristan of trying to hurt me when I knew, deep down he would never do such a thing. Slapping him just made me sound ungrateful. I wasn't sure I wanted to admit that to these females who insisted on using his formal title at all times.

"You want to hear what we know? I want to hear the story of how you upset the Winter Prince." Lainey leaned over my shoulder. "It seems to be the only story that isn't circulating right now.

What did you do to him that didn't make its way out to the rest of us?"

"You're really going to make me say it, aren't you?" I asked.

"It's been a long time since we've had anything entertaining happen around here," Lainey said with a shrug.

"There was an orc killed in the hallway last night. How much more entertaining did you need?" I asked.

Lainey waved her hand. "That's not entertainment, that's business. Give us something juicy we can enjoy for a while."

I felt my cheeks heating even more. It seemed, Lainey thought whatever I had done to upset Tristan was more intimate than I intended. "It's not that juicy."

She raised an eyebrow.

"Fine." I huffed. "When I was attacked, I thought maybe he was the one who had sent the assassin. So I slapped him. That's it."

Lainey and the other female looked at each other, a moment of silent understanding passing between them that I wasn't privy to. "What?"

"You attacked the Winter Prince?" Lainey asked. "That is not what I expected at all. I mean, I thought for sure the two of you snuck off somewhere together."

"I wouldn't call it an attack, exactly." Embarrassment surged through me. "It was a mistake. I was scared. I've apologized, but things still haven't returned to normal between the two of us." I reflected on those words and realized I had no idea what normal between Tristan and I even looked like. I hadn't known him very long, I hadn't known any of the princes that long. But Tristan and I seemed to exist on a different level than I did with the others.

"Who are you?" Lainey asked, dropping my hair back against my back. She grabbed the edge of the tub and stared at me, brow furrowed. The levity of our conversation was gone, replaced by something more serious.

"I told you, I'm no one important."

"No," Lainey said. "The last person who insulted the prince, was sentenced to death. He does not take betrayal lightly. The fact that you did that, in front of his entourage and his guards, I'm honestly surprised you're still alive."

"You can't be serious," I said, watching her expression. I expected it to break. For her to laugh and tell me that she was teasing me. But she didn't falter.

"You call him by his name, you insulted him, you assaulted him. You are someone very important," Lainey said.

A knock sounded on the door and the other girl promptly got up and scurried away to answer it.

I lowered my voice. "You're not going to tell anybody about this, are you?" I realize now that if she was telling the truth, this could be very dangerous for me and very difficult for Tristan to explain.

"As I said, everything that we say is private. We don't violate that rule here. We take very seriously."

The other girl returned and hovered above me next to the bathtub. In her hands, she held a bundle of clothing. "His Grace sent this for you. And like Lainey said, nothing leaves this room." She curtsied, averting her eyes. "My lady." Then she looked up and just the flicker of a smirk crossed her lips. "Or should I be calling you 'Your Grace'?"

My stomach turned at the thought of being given such a title. Tristan had offered for me to sleep in the suite designated for his wife, the one who would eventually wear that title. Then, he'd teased me by calling me a princess. Now, I find out the actions against him would have resulted in serious discipline for anyone who wasn't me.

Tristan came across as a flirt, but I didn't think there was anything other than sexual attraction between the two of us. Obviously, I was interested in him in that sense because who wouldn't be? But what if there was more to it than physical attraction?

# Chapter Sixteen

I thought of Ethan and I felt the weight of shame in the pit of my stomach. Hadn't we formed a mating bond? Didn't that mean I was his and he was mine? Thinking of Tristan in such a way seemed like I was betraying Ethan. And then there was Dane and even Cormac, who hated Tristan. I shook my head. "No, that's never going to happen. Tristan and I have nothing in common."

Lainey laughed. "If sex or even mating were just about the things you had in common, nobody would ever be with anyone. Trust me, Cassia, we've seen it all in here."

Jae held up a towel. "It doesn't really matter what you think you are to His Grace. Especially if you are, as you say, a nobody. He rules these lands. His word is law."

I blinked at Jae, not sure of how to respond to her. I knew he was the ruler of the Winter Court based on what I'd learned so far, but I never considered that he'd force me into anything I didn't want to do. Was I being naive? I frowned. I might not know him well, but I trusted him. I wasn't sure if that was a mistake, but I had to start somewhere with my intuition. "He's not like that."

"He is like that, Cassia," Lainey said, a look of concern drawn across her face. "He's been like that before. Please, be careful. Don't upset him."

I bit down on my lip to keep myself from saying anything more. Her words were making me question everything. If my judgment was this far off with him, could anything I'd done be trusted? I'd made a lot of choices in the last few days that I wouldn't have dreamed of making in the human realm. Even if Lainey was wrong, which I hoped she was, her warning wasn't lost on me. I needed to tread carefully in Faerie. There was too much I didn't know.

I stood, water rushing off of me back into the tub, then stepped onto a rug that had been placed on the ground.

Jae hurried over and draped the towel over my shoulders. I tugged it tighter around me, then turned to Lainey. "Thank you, I will heed your warning."

Lainey nodded once.

"Can you tell me what you know about the assassin now?" I asked.

She glanced over at Jae and the two of them seemed to exchange another silent conversation. Finally, she turned back to me and sighed. "There has been talk that the attack wasn't against you." She paused, glancing over at the door as if to make sure it was still closed. "They say it was intended for His Grace."

My chest tightened and I held my breath. Someone wanted to kill Tristan? The thought of anyone harming him made my heart ache. I wasn't sure where I stood with him, but I didn't want anything bad to happen to him. "Are you sure?"

"You can never share that," she said.

"I won't," I said. "But I need to know if you're sure."

"I'm sure."

My mouth went dry and I licked my lips and swallowed, trying to make the feeling go away. Tristan's nobles were calling in their armies and an assassin had been sent for him. This wasn't about me. There was mutiny in the air. Someone was trying to send him from him throne. "I have to see him."

"You need to put clothes on first," Jae said.

"Or not," Lainey said.

"Clothes," I agreed. "Then, I need to see him."

Jae insisted in rubbing rose oil on my bare skin before she'd let me put any clothes on. I stood as still as possible while feeling completely awkward as she rubbed the oil all over me. Between the rose petals in the bath, the rose soap, and the oil, I smelled as if I was sitting in the middle of a rose garden. "Is this normal?"

Jae paused, her hands on my thighs. "Oil after a bath? Of course. It keeps your skin soft."

"The roses," I clarified. "Is that a favorite scent?"

Jae finished rubbing in the oil on my legs, then stood to her full height. She rubbed the leftover oil onto her hands and up her bare arms. "Not that I've seen." She turned to Lainey. "How about you?"

"No," Lainey said. "Roses don't grow here. It's expensive stuff. We usually use almond or olive oil."

Jae blotted the excess oil from my skin with a fresh towel and I was left to wonder why I'd been set up with such luxury. There didn't seem to be a reason for most of the things that Tristan did. Maybe they wanted me to smell extra nice for the Queen's sister.

"This dress is stunning," Lainey said.

I turned to see her holding up a silver gown. It was long sleeved with an A-line skirt. Along the neckline was a row of white pearls and row of gray gems. The fabric shimmered in the flickering candlelight of the room as Lainey walked over to me.

It reminded me of the dress my sister had worn on my failed wedding day, only this one was even more beautiful. My jaw tightened as I remembered how quickly she'd dismissed Nani. She would have done the same thing to me.

Lainey held the dress out in front of me. Everything about this dress screamed Winter Court. It was a dress fit for a princess.

I frowned at the gown, hating the fact that I was being dressed up like a puppet for whatever plan Tristan had. We all were. Since we first entered the Winter Court, Tristan had been dressing all of us as if we were his entourage. The plan had been to take me to the Queen, yet, we were still here, in Tristan's home land. The dress was beautiful, but it reminded me that I was still between worlds. Not fully at home anywhere. Until I learned how to channel my magic and figured out where I came from, I was going to feel like I was make believe no matter how fine the gown was. "It is stunning."

Lainey and Jae helped me into the gown. Then, the two females chattered away while they worked on my hair. They seemed to have forgotten all the dangerous conversations we'd had in the last hour. But I couldn't focus on anything anymore. I was left wondering if Tristan was at risk and what the Queen's sister would want from me. It was overwhelming and confusing and I was ready to be as far away from royal politics as possible. The sooner we got this over with, the better. But first, I wanted to see Tristan. "Can you get me alone with Tristan?"

"I think we can handle that." She turned to Jae. "Think you can do that?"

"Of course I can." Without hesitation, she walked toward the door and slipped through it, closing it behind her.

"You be careful with him, alright?" Lainey said. "I know you have something different with him, but he's still who he is. That's never going to change. Not even his wife got him to fully let go of some of his ways."

"Like what?" I asked.

Just then the door opened and Lainey snapped her mouth shut and lowered her eyes. "Your Grace."

"Leave us."

The sound of his voice seemed to echo inside me, sending a vibration to my core.

Lainey curtseyed and after giving me a quick glance, she scurried away.

I swallowed and slowly turned to face Tristan. I'd been so desperate to see him, to make sure he was safe, that I hadn't thought about how I'd react to him once he was here.

"You wanted to see me?" Tristan asked.

"Thank you for coming," I said.

"I considered sending a message instead," he took a few steps closer to me, "but I am curious to see what you have to say to me while the others aren't around."

Tristan and I had spent some time alone over the past few days. Enough so that I knew that while he might get close to me, he had never done anything unwelcome or pushed too far. "I heard something. No one seems to want to tell me the answers. So far, you seem to be the only one who thinks I can handle knowing the truth. So I thought I'd ask you instead of listening to rumors."

"You know I'm going to ask who told you the rumor, don't you?" He moved even closer to me.

My pulse elevated with each step he took closer to me but I tried to ignore it. "You know I'm not going to tell you that."

He smirked. "You're deliciously loyal, Cassia. It's one of the qualities I admire about you."

He was standing so close to me now that I could nearly feel the heat of his body. My thighs clenched involuntarily at his closeness and I forced myself to focus. "I heard a rumor about the assassin's target."

"I agreed with Cormac this time, that the details weren't necessary for your ears." He narrowed his eyes and seemed to study my face. "But I think he underestimated you. Not a mistake I'm about to make. Yes, the assassin wasn't meant for you. And yes, some of my nobles called in their troops. I can see you working out the pieces, that brain of yours, with the Autumn hunter mentality. Puzzling it all together. Honestly, if it weren't for the strategies those Autumn hunters can come up with, the Winter Court would have succeeded in taking over rather than leaving the other courts behind."

"So that's what happened?" I asked, relishing the new piece of information I'd obtained about Faerie's past.

"Yes, that's part of what Cormac doesn't want you to know. However, that doesn't matter to us now."

"What's going on here, Tristan?" I asked.

"I'm not sure yet, but I have a feeling we're heading to war again. And this time, I'm not on the inside. But when I have more information, I'll let you know. I don't see why you have to be kept in the dark," he said.

"Why not just tell me that? Why let me think someone was after me?" I asked.

"Because some of them are after you, Princess," Tristan said.

I frowned at his use of the word *princess* again. "I'm not a Princess."

"With all the time you've been spending with those princes, it's likely only a matter of time." Tristan shrugged. He didn't seem jealous in the slightest, an observation that made my stomach turn. For some reason, I wanted him to feel that way. To be a little bit upset about what I had with the others.

"You realized none of this makes sense. Why keep me in the dark? As you said yourself, I can put the pieces together. I can help."

"No, you can't. Not right now, anyway," he said.

"But-"

Tristan put his hand up, interrupting my objection. "There's something you should know about the Queen's sister," Tristan said. "They're half-sisters, two different fathers. One of them, was Winter Fae. She's gifted at reading minds. Probably the most gifted I've ever met."

"Is that something all the Winter Fae can do?" It was something I'd wondered about for a while since meeting Angela.

"No," Tristan said. "Some of us have the gift of sight instead. Some of us have none of those gifts."

He cocked his head to the side and furrowed his brow. "Do you have either of those gifts?"

I swallowed, not sure how to answer that question. I'd had flashes of moments that felt so real that I wondered if they were the future. But I didn't know what any of it meant yet. "I'm not sure."

"Interesting," Tristan said. "Well, whatever you're hiding from me and the others is about to come out. Tiana is very thorough."

I clenched my jaw, trying not to show Tristan that I was nervous about anyone reading my mind.

"We shouldn't keep her waiting. Was there anything else you needed from me?" he asked.

"Are you safe?" The words tumbled out before I could think them through.

Tristan laughed. "Am I safe? Why would you care?"

I crossed my arms over my chest. "Maybe I worry about you, alright?"

"You accused me of trying to kill you," he said.

"And I said I was sorry. I meant it. Why can't you believe that I'd be worried about you when I hear that your nobles are plotting against you and someone broke in here to kill you?"

"You know," he said. "You're the first female I've ever met who turned me down."

I stood in stunned silence. Was that what this was all about? My refusal to sleep in his chambers? I opened my mouth to say something but Tristan already had the door open.

"We're late, princess. Time to go."

Pursing my lips, I marched through the open door into the hall. Tristan had a way of making me feel like I wanted to simultaneously scream at him and tear his clothes off. It was one of the most infuriating and confusing feelings I'd ever had.

Worried I'd betray more than I wanted, I silently followed him down the hall.

I had a mind reader to meet and I hoped she'd keep everything she found in my head to herself.

# Chapter Seventeen

I followed Tristan up the stairs and down the hall on the fourth floor. As we approached the room I had just left, I saw Cormac, Ethan, and Dane waiting in the hall. Beyond them, two guards that weren't wearing the colors of the Winter Court were standing on either side of the now closed door. I stared at their burgundy and gold uniforms, trying to place where they came from. Were they traveling as envoys of the Autumn Court or were they directly from the Queen's palace?

"You do look like a princess, love," Dane said.

I lifted an eyebrow in silent protest.

"The colors of the Winter Court look especially stunning on her, don't you think?" Tristan asked.

"She'd look good in anything," Ethan said.

"That's probably true," Tristan said. "Look at us, agreeing on something."

"That is nice to see for a change," I said.

The only male standing in silence was Cormac. His gaze seemed fixated somewhere beyond me as if he wasn't even seeing me.

"Everything alright, Cormac?" I asked, my brow furrowed in concern.

He blinked and then looked at me, as if seeing me for the first time since I arrived. "I'm fine. Lots to think about."

I'd seen Cormac walk away to sulk or be alone. I'd never seen him lose focus in front of me. It was concerning to say the least. "You sure?"

"You should be worried about yourself right now, not me," he said.

"She'll be fine," Ethan said. "I'm sure she'll dazzle her."

My stomach twisted into knots as I realized the Queen's sister was here waiting for me. How did one respond to the sister of a queen? Especially in a place where the title is earned through a trial instead of birth?

"We'll be right outside, Love," Dane said.

"You're not going to see her with me?" Suddenly, my mouth felt very dry.

"She's requested an audience with you alone," Cormac said. "You have nothing to fear."

"Except for any secrets you don't want us to know," Tristan said.

"Cassia," Ethan said. "You have nothing to worry about because you have nothing to hide."

I swallowed and nodded slowly. I hoped I had nothing to hide, but I didn't know enough about who I was or what I was doing here to know what was right or wrong. Was the magic I had going to cause trouble for me? Was my relationship with these males in danger or had I endangered them? Would she now be able to tell how confused I was about everything?

The door opened and another guard stepped out. His burgundy and gold uniform looked so bright against the stark grays and whites of the Winter Court.

I glanced at the princes, wishing I had thought to ask questions that were useful.

"She's ready for you," the guard said.

I turned back to the door as a weight settled into my body, making each step more difficult than it should be. Slowly, I walked toward the door. I didn't look back at any of the princes. I was afraid that I'd lose my nerve if I did. Or that I'd have another one of the strange sexual encounters flash into my mind in front of the mind reader.

I stepped through the threshold and stopped a few steps away from the double doors. Two chairs had been brought into the nearly empty room while I'd been dressing. One was occupied by a female in a gold dress. She stood when she saw me, sending the iridescent fabric of her dress rippling in the weak afternoon sun. She was a few inches taller than me and had long, curly blonde hair that cascaded down her back.

Expression serious, the female seemed to examine me with her blue eyes. Her sharp, pointed nose moved up and down as she made no attempt to mask her thorough examination of me.

I swallowed against a lump in my throat and clenched my hands together as I waited for her to speak.

She walked in a circle around me, the only sound the gentle whisper of fabric over the wood floor.

After what felt like minutes of silence, she walked back to the chair she had been occupying, and sat down. Then, she gestured to the chair opposite hers. "Please, sit."

I sat down in the chair across then remembered my manners. I bolted up so I could drop into a curtsey. All of my informal time with the princes had caused me to forget protocol. "Forgive me, Your Grace."

"Sit, girl. There's no one to see us in here. Besides, I'm not the Queen. I hold no royal titles. I was born into nobility, yes. But I doubt I'm any more high-ranking than you."

"I'm not sure where I would rank." I sat back down, thinking about how nice it would be to sink into anonymity somewhere.

"You really don't care, do you?" She leaned back in the chair and stretched her long arms along the armrests, wrapping slender fingers around the end. She tilted her head and narrowed her eyes, inspecting me again. "It's rare to meet someone who doesn't worry about such things as rank. Truly, you seem like you'd almost rather be a nobody."

I wasn't sure what to say. All of her comments were true, of course. But I hadn't said anything that would make her come to those conclusions. Was she already reading my mind? "I wasn't born here, or at least I wasn't raised here I mean, I suppose I was born here. Somewhere in Faerie at least. But I didn't even know I was Fae until a few days ago."

She lifted a hand and waved dismissively at me. "I know all that. Cormac told me everything. How they found you, the attack at your wedding, the fact that your father was paid off by someone. I'm here to figure out if your powers might give us a clue as to who sent you to that horrid place to begin with."

I leaned back in the chair, considering her words. She probably knew the whole tale of my time with the princes. She probably knew of the attacks by the monsters and how we hunted them. It was possible she even knew about my relationships with two of them. "We were on our way to see the Queen." The words sounded stupid as they came out of my mouth, but I didn't know what else to say.

"I'm aware. I'm also aware of the fact that you show an affinity for three, maybe even four Courts. That's something that shouldn't be possible. Even our strongest, most elite warriors do not have affinity for more than one Court. Those like me, born of two Courts only hold the power of one. There have been stories of those who have carried the powers of both their mother and father, but they've never been proven as true. For you to have all four is impossible. Unless..." she trailed off, then pushed herself to standing.

"Unless what?" I asked.

She moved on silent footsteps until she closed the distance

between the two of us. My heart raced, as I sat glued to the space in the chair staring up at the female. I could tell she was dangerous, it wasn't even a question in my mind. I knew this was someone you did not want to cross.

She stretched her arms out until her hands were hovering on either side of my head. "Don't worry, this won't hurt." She gently touched her fingertips to my temples and then she closed her eyes.

For a moment, I watched her eyelids flicker, wondering what she was doing to me. Then, I gasped as my body involuntarily pressed harder into the back of the chair. I winced, as something uncomfortable withered through me, rolling down my spine and crawling up through my limbs toward my head. It didn't hurt, exactly. But it was uncomfortable and I strained against the unnatural intrusion.

I wanted to free myself from her, I wanted to get out of the chair and run from the room into the safety of Dane or Ethan or Cormac or even Tristan. I tried to scream, but sound wouldn't escape my mouth.

Terrified, I squirmed, trying to break free of the chair. My body was stuck, frozen in place, as if bound by invisible chains. Searing heat sizzled across my skin as a memory replayed in my mind. I was trying to escape my father's home and in the white light I had created, someone had bound me with chains. The pain coursed through my body as if I were really there. When I broke free in the memory, relief surged through me as I made my escape.

The memory was gone only to be replaced by another. I was standing next to Cormac in front of a bonfire and a rush of emotions tumbled through me. Want, desire, sadness, pain, hunger. They mixed into a boiling pool and despite the fact that I knew it was a memory, I reached for Cormac trying to grab hold of him to pull myself out of whatever nightmare I'd been sucked into. As I reached for him, he faded, only to be replaced by Ethan with his arms around me.

I only got the touch of him for a second before that happy memory was ripped from me, sending me into the last monster attack where I had to watch all four of the males I had grown to care about fighting for their lives. I screamed, opening my mouth without sound. I didn't want to relive this memory. I didn't want to see Ethan hurt again. I didn't want to go back to that place where I was unsure if he would live or die. As the battle played out in front of me, I fought against the invisible restraints until I felt the clawing of my own magic inside.

Mentally, I reached for my magic, pulling on it, encouraging it. I wanted out of whatever this was and I was willing to do whatever it took to make it stop. Something felt like it exploded inside of me and I launched myself from the chair, finally regaining control of my body. I landed in a heap on the floor, my breathing rapid as if I had been running for miles.

Slowly, I rolled onto my back and looked up at where Tiana was staring down at me eyes wide in surprise.

I sat up and pushed myself to standing. "That memory is not for you. I am not going to live through almost losing Ethan. Do you understand me?" I knew I shouldn't be threatening her. I knew she was more powerful than anyone I'd encountered so far. Probably more powerful than any of the princes waiting outside the door for me. But I didn't know her, and I was willing to risk her wrath to keep from having to go through that pain again. "You have no right."

"Sit down." The words came out like a command.

I knew I pushed it too far, I didn't have Cormac here to protect me and for all I knew, insulting the Queen's sister could be the same as insulting the Queen herself.

Lower lip trembling I tried to remain calm. I wanted to show her I was strong and that I wasn't someone to be pushed around.

"You don't belong inside my head. If there's something you want to know, ask me."

"Sit." She backed away from me, settling into the chair across from me again.

Slowing my breathing, I forced myself to sit. My hands were shaking with anger as I stared at the stranger. Why would she do that to me? Why would she put me through that again? What did she need from my head? Jaw clenched, I forced myself to remain silent while I waited for an explanation.

## Chapter Eighteen

✦

"You do have some magic," she said. "And it's strong enough to push me out of your head."

"You already knew that. I told you. You could have asked me," I said.

"I was hoping to be able to identify your magic from your memories. But since you won't grant me access to them, which I must admit is a pretty impressive feat for someone who says she had no training, we'll have to do it a different way."

"I haven't had any training. Cormac started showing me how to cycle, but that's it," I said. "Wait, what other way?"

"You have to be tested. I can't allow you to visit my sister until I know what you're capable of. If you won't let me see your memories, we'll have to do something else."

"It might've gone better if you told me what you were doing. I've never had someone inside my head before. I was scared."

"Oh really?" she said with a smirk. "You've been around Tristan for the last several days and you have no ability to mask what you're thinking. His skills are almost as good as my own. I guarantee you, he's seen inside your head."

Tristan had told me he couldn't see my future, but I didn't

know what all he was capable of. I was transported back to that moment in a small palace where I pictured Tristan naked. He commented in a way that made me know he'd seen what I was thinking. Flushed, hoping the female seated in front of me couldn't read my thoughts. But now I didn't know what to believe. "Seeing memories is different from seeing what people are thinking?"

"Yes," she said. "Not everyone who can read thoughts can access memories. As you now know, the process can be uncomfortable for the person who's having memories read. Though, to be fair, I had no way of knowing you had such painful memories."

"Like I said, you never asked." I crossed my arms over my chest. We were going in circles and I was starting to think this was exactly what Tiana wanted. I didn't know what her other method of testing powers was, but she seemed rather pleased that I had kicked her out of my head.

"I'm surprised the princes have agreed to help you with a mouth like that. If I found you, and you spoke to me this way, I would've thrown you to the beasts. You must be a very good partner in bed. There's no other reason I can think of that they keep you around."

Heat rose in my chest and I tightened my hands into fists. "I suppose I should be grateful that it wasn't you who found me."

"If it weren't for Cormac's protection, I'd have you thrown out now. Like I said, being sister to the Queen doesn't afford me any rank privileges so Cormac as Prince of the Autumn Court, holds greater power than I do. However, without my blessing, you'll never get to see the Queen."

"I'm not trying to cause trouble here, I just want to find out how to control the magic I have."

"You do realize, if you can control magic from multiple courts, it will make you nearly equal in power to the Queen herself. Why would anyone want a rival like that?" she asked.

I swallowed, not knowing how to respond to that. I wasn't

sure how I could convince her I wasn't a threat. Tiana liked to turn my words against me. I bit down on the inside of my cheek to keep from commenting. She was playing games with me. Toying with me. And if I wasn't careful, I'd do something that would cause me to lose.

Tiana stood and lifted her chin high. I knew she was making a show of looking down on me. "I need to rest before I can perform the test. After the evening meal, you and I will meet back here alone. Then, I can find out once and for all the kind of magic you have. And if you can learn to control your tongue, perhaps I will give you my blessing to visit my sister."

She walked toward the door, her gold dress leaving a shimmering puddle of fabric in her wake. When she reached the door, she turned back and looked at me. "There are those who have died having their magic tested. If you are hiding anything from me, you'll want to confess before we begin."

I kept my face expressionless as she turned from me to open the large set of double doors. As soon as she walked through, I collapsed into the chair, lower lip trembling, my mind a swirling mass of confusion.

I had managed to completely offend the one person I should have been trying to impress. I knew it was my own fault. I knew I should've kept my mouth shut. I couldn't help it. I didn't want to be pushed around by anyone anymore and I was tired of being the last to know everything.

What kind of test was she going to give me that had caused others to die? Was that even legal?

How was I supposed to demonstrate to someone that I wasn't a threat? Even with the ability to control the magic of all four Courts, I had no intention of using it. My dream was to live a simple life somewhere where I could make my own choices about what I did each day. I had no ambition of attacking anyone or fighting anyone or taking anyone's kingdom. Why couldn't she see that?

Footsteps sounded in the room I turned to see Cormac entering alone. The doors closed behind him and I straightened in the chair, ready to be disciplined by the prince I had let down. I was under his protection, and when I did something that made me look bad, I knew it made him look bad too. That wasn't my intention. Like a child who knew she'd gone too far, my shoulders sank and I looked down at my hands folded in my lap.

"I'm so sorry. She made me re-live the attack. The one where Ethan nearly died. I couldn't take it."

"She made up her mind about you before she even saw you. No matter what you said, she was going to find an excuse to test you," Cormac said. "I just didn't realize it until she spoke to me just now."

Gently, Cormac touched my chin with his finger and lifted it so I was looking up into his eyes. "You're going to be fine. We have a few hours before the test, we'll help you prepare."

Grateful that he wasn't upset with me I nodded. "It's my fault, though. I pushed her out of my mind."

Cormac's brow furrowed. "You pushed her out?"

"Yes. I know I shouldn't have, but I wasn't sure what she was doing until I'd already pushed her away."

"It's impressive that you were able to push her out." He smiled. "I'm sure she hated that."

"She did," I said.

"Listen, Cassia." Cormac sighed. "We have a long history with Tiana. All of us. If it's anyone's fault, it's mine. But I don't want you to worry, you'll do fine on the test. We know you have the magic that's required to pass it."

"How could it be your fault?" I asked. "You've done nothing but help me. I could never blame you for anything. This is on me."

He brushed a loose strand of hair away from my eyes. "Trust me on this, Cassia. You're not the one to blame here. Tiana has always had a vindictive streak. We were in the Academy together.

Ethan, Dane, and I. And I guarantee you she did some digging in our heads before she came to see you." Cormac dropped to his knees in front of me. And took both of my hands in his. "She knows you're important to all of us, and she knows that if she hurts you it hurts us."

"That doesn't make any sense. What could any of you have possibly done to make her so angry?" I asked.

"She and her sister both wanted a bid for Queen's Trial. Each house can only have one champion and she asked us to choose her over her sister. But I know Tiana too well and having her on the throne was not a good idea. She was close with Dane back then and even managed to fool Ethan. But I saw right through her and when it came time to throw our support behind the champions, I was able to convince both Dane and Ethan to side with me against her."

"So all of this goes back to Queen's Trial?" Everything seemed to connect to this. The sooner I could get away from the drama of the Court, the better. "Why would she hold on to the grudge for so long? Surely, she can't still be upset by this?" I asked.

"As I said, she has a vindictive streak. I thought she'd let it go, but apparently not. Now that I think of it, it wouldn't surprise me if she's been waiting until she could find a way to punish us all at the same time and through you, she found a way to do it."

My chest was tight and my heart heavy as Cormac's words sank in. I didn't want to cause this much trouble for him or any of them. "Maybe I should just run away. Is there somewhere I can just hide until this whole Queen's Trial thing blows over?"

Cormac chuckled. "You wouldn't last a day out there on your own without being able to control that magic of yours. You're like a beacon for anything trying to make its way out of the Under."

"Cormac, I'm sorry. I didn't mean for any of this to happen. I'm sorry that I dragged you all into this."

Cormac stood, still holding onto my hands and he yanked me up so I was standing next to him. "No more apologizing to me.

Not ever. I chose to take you under my protection. Dane chose to take you into his bed. Ethan told me he thinks he feels the mating bond with you. None of us are going anywhere."

Hot tears stung the back of my eyes and I blinked to try and keep them from streaking down my face. My whole life, I wanted to feel like I belonged. I wanted to feel like I mattered to someone. It turned out, I mattered more than I ever thought I could to three princes that I felt the same way about. Wiping a stray tear off my cheek I took a deep breath in. "Tell me how to survive this test. I won't let you down."

"The most important thing is to be completely focused. No lingering guilt, no lingering anger, no unresolved problems. I need your mind sharp. Whatever it is that's in your head right now that's causing you any kind of turmoil, you need to let it go. Tiana will see emotions as weakness and she'll be able to use them against you. She shouldn't, but she will."

The door swung open and Cormac and I turned to see Ethan walking in with a tray of food.

"No way were letting her take a test on an empty stomach." Ethan set the tray down on the large table, pushing away some of the scrolls and little objects to make space for it.

"Thank you," I said, my stomach growling in response to the smell of food. I glanced to the open door, half expecting Dane to walk in and say something cocky. But he didn't. "Where's Dane?"

"Nowhere," Ethan said.

I glanced at Cormac them back to Ethan. "No more lies. If you want me to have a clear head for this trial, you have to be honest with me."

"She's right," Cormac said.

Ethan's shoulders sank. "You're not going to like it."

"Just tell me," I said.

Ethan glanced at Cormac again before looking back at me. "He's with Tiana, trying to put her in a better mood before the test."

## Chapter Nineteen

"You can't be serious," I said. "She's a nightmare. How could he do anything with her?" What I wanted to ask was how could he do that to me? How could he be with me one night and then turn around and be with someone like her the next night? My insides clenched as I realized that was the exact same thing I had done to him. Was this his way of getting back at me? Perhaps it was his way of telling me or showing me he needed more than just me or that he wasn't happy with Ethan and me.

"He couldn't," Dane's voice carried to the large room.

My heart leapt and I looked over to see him standing in the doorway. I smiled, then ran over to him. "What happened?"

"Oddly, for the first time, I'm happy with one female in my life. I don't need anyone else." Dane hugged me and kissed the top of my head before letting go of me. "The problem is, I probably only made her more angry. Whatever Cormac can teach you about this test, you need to learn it."

"I feel so left out," Tristan said.

"Well, it looks like the gang's all here," Dane said.

"I take it didn't go well," Tristan said.

"That's not helping, Tristan," Ethan said.

"I'm not sure why you're going to have Cormac work with her. Out of all of us in this room, I'm the only one that's ever gone through the magic test. Granted, I didn't make Tiana angry before she gave it to me, but I may have better insight for Cassia than anyone else." Tristan leaned against the door jamb and crossed his arms casually over his chest.

"Have you really been through it?" I asked.

"I have. My crazy father insisted on having all of his children tested. Poor bastard hoped he would end up with offspring who have the powers from more than one court. It's why we all have different mothers. He kept trying with new women all the time."

I had never heard Tristan talk about siblings before and wondered where the other princes or princesses of the Winter Court were.

"She told me people sometimes die when they take this test," I said.

"A human would die," Tristan said. "Or half-breed. Someone born half of the human realm and half of our realm. Someone with only one court of magic might die, I suppose. I don't think we need to worry about that with you. Based on what we've seen so far, your magic is possibly going to be strong enough that you would be a threat to the Queen herself."

"That's something Tiana mentioned. She said something about how if I have all four powers it makes me dangerous to the Queen. But you know I would never hurt anyone," I said.

"That's not true, Princess," Tristan said. "We've seen you fight when you feel like you're threatened or when someone you love is threatened." Tristan looked over at Ethan then back at me. "She probably saw that when she looked at your memories. She knows you're a fighter and she doesn't know whose side you're on. The best way for you to survive this, is to make her think you're on her side."

"Isn't she on the same side as the Queen? Isn't that the side I would just be on?" I asked.

"Unless you're Winter Fae," Ethan said.

"I don't think she is Winter," Tristan said. "But I'd be willing to make an exception and allow her to stay if she chose."

"She's not staying with you, Tristan," Cormac said. "And all we're doing right now is wasting time. She has hours left before the test and she needs to prepare."

"Why don't you let her choose for herself, then?" Tristan asked. "She can prepare with me, the only one in this room that has seen what the test entails, or she can train with you, the mighty Prince of the Autumn Court. Favorite to the Queen, war hero, soldier with thousands of confirmed kills."

I looked back over at Cormac, my brow furrowed. "Kills? I thought you were a hunter."

"I told you, Princess. Hunters make the best warriors," Tristan said.

"No need to make her choose," Cormac said. "I want what's best for her. And if you think your knowledge of this test can help her get through it unharmed, you should be the one to do it."

I could almost feel Cormac retreating into himself again. I'd seen him do it so many times before. It was as if I could feel him closing himself off. "Cormac, don't." I wasn't sure how to explain what I wanted to tell him or what I wanted to ask him. How did you explain to such a proud male that you were there for him? Especially when he wouldn't let you in?

"Tristan, this is serious," Ethan said. "She might not die from the test, but we all know there are other consequences that could happen. Can you do this?"

"I made a promise to Cassia," Tristan glanced at me then looked back to Ethan, "I keep my promises."

"I'll wait outside the door if you need me," Ethan said, grabbing my hand and giving it a squeeze.

I squeezed him back, but didn't have any words to offer as he released my hand and walked from the room, followed by Dane and Cormac. The door closed behind them and I once again found myself alone with Tristan.

"Why do you do that?" I asked.

"Do what?" he asked.

"Say things just to upset Cormac. You knew how he'd react to your words," I said.

"Princess, you have to realize, he's not the golden one you think he is. He's got his share of demons. We all do. Well, maybe not Ethan. He's probably the most adorable of all of us. The rest of us, we're no good for you."

I scowled at him. "I don't need anyone telling me who is or isn't good for me."

He shrugged. "I know you'll never listen to reason, you're in too deep already."

"What's that supposed to mean?" I asked.

"You know what it means. But now isn't the time to argue. Ethan was right. This isn't a game. And we're running out of time to help you prepare."

"We're going to talk more later," I said.

"We will," he agreed. "After the test."

I wanted to press on, to understand what was going on inside Tristan's head, but we were losing time. "What exactly is it? The test?"

"Only those who've been through the test truly know what it entails and while you won't die from it, there have been several cases of Fae driven mad by the elements of the test. Most of the time that happens when someone is tested for all four courts of magic. Which is what she's going to do to you. The difference is, I think the madness stems from being tested for magic you don't possess in the slightest. We know you have at least three, possibly four of the courts worth of magic flowing through you. So I doubt you'll walk away from it with too much damage, but we have to be smart about this."

I glanced around the larger than necessary room. Looking for a distraction, anything to take my mind off of the thought of the looming test. I wondered if it would be easier to hear all of this and face my fears if I had Ethan or Dane by my side. I looked back at Tristan. "Why do we have to be alone for this?"

"Because my methods are unconventional."

A trickle of fear ran down my spine. I still didn't know everything responsible for Tristan's dark reputation. I tried to remind myself that the others would not have left me alone with him if they were worried he would harm me. But I still couldn't imagine what Tristan wanted to do that he wouldn't want the others to see.

"At some point, you're going to have to learn how to trust me. Or this isn't going to work." Tristan looked hurt. "I'm trusting you by helping you with this."

The fear I was feeling gave way to guilt. I wanted to trust him. "What is it that we need to do then? I'll do my best."

"What I'm going to do for you has to remain between the two of us. You can't tell the others. You can't tell anyone."

I swallowed hard. "I don't understand what you'd want me to keep from them. Besides, won't Tiana find out when I meet with her?"

"I'm hoping she'll be more focused on administering the test than digging through your head." Tristan crossed the room toward the two chairs, sat, then gesture to one of them. "This is the best way. If you want to be successful."

Squaring my shoulders, I walked over to the chair and sat. "I won't tell. You have my word."

Tristan knelt in front of me just as Cormac had when he'd come to comfort me after my meeting with Tiana. The sight of the Winter Prince on his knees in front of me was enough to send a rush of lust surging through me. To be honest, I never thought I'd see Tristan on his knees in front of anyone. Least of all me. I shouldn't keep feeling like this about him. What was it about Tristan that made me feel like I wanted to lose all control?

Squeezing my thighs together, I took a few deep breaths, hoping he couldn't sense my arousal.

Tristan lifted his fingers to my temples, just as Tiana had done. "I'm going to try and reduce any pain that comes with these memories, but I can't mask it all. You'll need to try to stay quiet. I don't want Ethan or Dane crashing in on us."

"I don't want you digging through my memories." My heart raced and I fidgeted in the chair, ready to push myself past him toward the door if needed. I didn't want to go through that again. Feeling someone else inside my head wasn't pleasant. I was still haunted by Tiana poking around at things I didn't want to see again.

"These won't be your memories. They belong to someone else. As far as I know, I'm the only one who has this gift and no one else knows I can do this. I need you to help me keep it that way."

Understanding why Tristan wanted to do this in secret now, I nodded.

"Close your eyes and try not to fight it." He pressed his fingertips gently against my temples. "I'll be right here the whole time."

I closed my eyes and forced myself to steady my breathing, overly aware of Tristan's fingers against my skin. His touch was cooling and more comforting than I expected it to be. I settled my hands in my lap and waited, anticipation prickling up and down my arms.

All at once, the blackness of the back of my eyelids was replaced by watery, fading sunlight. I recognized the sitting room of Tristan's palace where we spent the night before embarking on this journey to the Queen. There were two figures seated on the couch. One of them small, a child. The other an older female who looked only a few years younger than me. They both had the same blonde hair and the same icy blue eyes. Dressed in the colors of the Winter Court, I knew these had to be important people in Tristan's family. Was the young boy one of his siblings? And who was the female?

Footsteps from behind me caused the two figures to look up and I saw the color drain from the boy's face. I turned to see who the newcomer was and my breath hitched at the sight of Tiana striding into the room as if she owned the place. Still dressed in gold, this time in a long flowing gold tunic over tight wine colored leggings. Her boot heels clicked across the wood floor as she approached the waiting Fae.

She stopped in front of them and looked down at the boy, narrowing her eyes at him. "So this is young Tristan? Not quite what I expected for someone rumored to have magic that rivals my own."

I tensed and took a silent step closer to the young version of the Winter Prince. This scared boy looked nothing like the confident male I'd come to know. And who was the female with him? Where was she now?

The female put her arm protectively around the young Tristan. "Tristan, this is Lady Tiana. She will administer the test. Don't be nervous, we all had to take it when we were your age."

"Will you wait here with me, Sasha?" young Tristan asked.

Sasha shook her head. "I have to go help Mother. But when you're finished, I have a surprise for you. I asked the cook to make your favorite sweet cakes. They'll be ready when you're done."

Sasha kissed Tristan on the forehead, then stood. "Lady Tiana." She curtsied toward Tiana and the older Fae inclined her head. "Princess."

Sasha walked away, but lingered at the door. It seemed like she wanted to say something else. After a heartbeat longer hesitation, she didn't even look back at Tristan. She walked from the room until she was out of sight, leaving Tristan alone with Tiana.

Tiana took the vacant seat on the couch next to Tristan. "Has anyone told you anything about the test?" she asked.

Young Tristan shook his head. "Only that Father expects that I'll do well."

"I never expect anyone to do well. It's so rare to find a Fae who has magic beyond normal capacity. If anything, I often find those that request the tests have less magic than they should. Too many overindulgent parents who think their offspring are special. Do you think that's the case with you?"

"I don't know," Tristan said. "I've rarely even see my father."

Tiana's lips twisted as she pondered his words. "Well, you are the seventh son."

"So they remind me every day," Tristan said.

"I'm sure they do." Tiana sat quietly for a moment, watching the prince. Finally, she adjusted her position and turned closer to him. "Shall we begin?"

Young Tristan fixed a determined expression on his face, tightening his jaw. He nodded once, but didn't speak.

I could almost feel his fear as he tried to remain strong despite the very intimidating female in front of him.

She extended her hands palms up. "Place your hands on top of mine."

Tristan reached out, his fingers trembling slightly as he set his palms against hers.

I narrowed my eyes, watching Tiana closely. What was she doing? How was she going to test him by nearly holding hands?

I gasped as shimmering gold threads wrapped their way around their hands, binding them together. The threads shimmered and glowed, continuing to wrap themselves around their hands, seemingly coming from nowhere.

Young Tristan grunted and I looked over at his face. His nose was scrunched up and his teeth were clenched. Whatever these threads were doing, pain was part of it. He seemed to be fighting against something internally and he winced as his hands began to shake. It almost seemed like he was trying to force himself from pulling his hands away.

I looked at Tiana, horrified to find that she was smiling. I glared at her, hating her for what she was doing to the prince. I could tell she was enjoying every second of discomfort she was causing for her young victim.

My heart ached I stood there silently observing the scene while the young Tristan started to squirm. I felt so helpless, but I knew this was a memory, it wouldn't be possible for me to intervene.

A sharp echo of pain scraped against my hand, then traveled up my arms to my head. I winced and looked at my hand, there was nothing visibly wrong with me.

The pain intensified, and my vision blurred. Was I feeling the pain Tristan was experiencing?

Tristan cried out the same time as a fresh pain jabbed into my skull. My breathing was shallow as I fought against the invasion in my head. Pain trickled down into my neck and into my shoulders, then found its way through the rest of my limbs, making it difficult to stand.

I closed my eyes and took a deep breath, telling myself none of this was real, but the pain felt real. Finally, in a rush of relief, I felt a release as the pain disappeared all at once.

I snapped my eyes open and looked over at young Tristan to find the gold threads were no longer wrapped around their hands. Tristan had fallen back against the couch, breathing heavy. A sheen of sweat shone on his forehead and strands of his blonde hair stuck to the perspiration. He took a few more breaths, then straightened, fixing his gaze back on Tiana. His nostrils flared but he didn't speak.

Tiana wore the smile of a predator watching the injured and weak member of the herd. Anger surged through me as I stared at her wide, toothy grin. No one should be this happy from inflicting pain on another. Tiana was a monster.

"You have no affinity for magic of the Autumn Court. One disappointment so far," Tiana said. "Shall we continue or are you ready to give up?"

"Continue," Tristan said through gritted teeth.

"Very well," she said, stretching her hands out for him again.

This time, when Tristan set his hand on top of hers he was no longer shaking. He was either in too much pain to be nervous this time, or the fear had given way to anger.

Just like before, threads began to wind their way around the pair of hands. Only this time, they were pink and shimmered with an iridescent quality that almost made them look purple at times. If gold had been the color of the Autumn Court, this had to be either Summer or Spring. I had a feeling, the Winter Court would be silver. I also had a feeling that Tiana was saving the Winter Court for last. She was going to put him through all three of the other Courts before she tested him for the magic he most likely had.

My jaw tightened as I watched the young Tristan grimace against the oncoming pain. I could tell he was fighting through it, his entire body tense. A bead of sweat dripped down his face as he forced his gaze to maintain eye contact with Tiana. He was so young, only a child, yet there was a power behind him that couldn't be ignored. I wondered if it was that power that Tiana was trying to break.

The pain came on in a gust this time hitting my entire body so hard I nearly toppled over. Gasping, I fought against hundreds of tiny pinpricks of pain up and down my body. I felt like I was rolling in a pile of needles and it took everything I had not to scream. I clamped my jaw shut and bawled my hands into fists, fighting against it. If the young child in front of me could do it, I could too.

# Chapter Twenty

I fought to keep my eyes open this time, wanting to see how Tristan reacted to this fresh round of pain. I could see how this could cause madness in someone. Especially if the grown Tristan was diluting the pain as much as he could for me. I couldn't imagine what it felt like to the young boy in the memory. How had he gone through all of this? And why?

The young prince swayed, and for a moment I feared he was going to pass out. Then, Tristan let out a noise that was somewhere between a growl and scream and he fought to remain seated. Finally, the pain vanished and the pink strands around his hands faded.

Tiana crossed her legs and cocked her head to the side, inspecting the panting boy in front of her. Tristan was leaned forward, forearms on his knees, head drooping. His hair was slick with sweat now and dark circles had formed under his eyes. After a few heartbeats of breath, the young Tristan looked up at Tiana. "That it?"

I couldn't help but smile at his defiance. The boy who had started the session seemed timid and insecure and now I was staring at a changed male. This was the Tristan I knew. The

Tristan who didn't let people push him around the Tristan who didn't care what people thought. The Tristan who fought for what he wanted.

Tiana frowned and uncrossed her legs. Without a word, she extended her hands palm up. "I was going to move to Winter next to give you a break, but it seems your spirit could use a little reminder of who's in charge here."

"You'll never be in charge here, you'll never be in charge anywhere. I heard you lost your bid for Queen's Trial."

Tiana squeezed Tristan's hands as green threads wrapped around them. I braced myself to feel the pain of whatever was coming and watched Tristan's reaction.

Tristan straightened his posture and locked his eyes on Tiana. The green ribbons around their hands continued to grow, increasing in thickness and number until the strands started to climb up Tristan's wrist and up his arms. Tristan smirked and I felt a flicker of hope rise in my chest. I wasn't feeling any pain and Tristan didn't look like he was experiencing any. The winding tendrils grew brighter as the green gave way, shifting to orange until they began to break free of the organized strands. Wisps of orange and yellow climbed wildly up Tristan's arms.

Stunned, my eyes widened as I realized the glowing colors weren't the same threads I'd seen before. What started out as green ribbons had transformed into fire. Perfect spirals of tiny flickering flames wrapped around Tristan's arms spreading from his wrists up to Tiana's.

Tiana yelped and pulled her hands away from Tristan breaking the connection. The fire continued to burn on Tristan for a few seconds longer before it faded.

"I see your father got his wish," Tiana said. "A Winter Fae with Summer magic." She stood. "No need to test your Winter magic. I could feel you probing my mind the second I walked into the room. You're lucky, last time I tested one of your siblings, he didn't leave the room in one piece."

Tristan stood, his hands balling into fists and his gaze boring daggers into Tiana. But he didn't speak, he didn't comment at Tiana's attempt to rile him up.

"Perhaps," Tiana said flashing a wicked grin, "there will be a strong ruler one day in the Winter Court after all."

Blackness returned and I gasped as my eyes fluttered open. I looked at the grown Tristan in front of me feeling a deeper understanding of who he was and what he'd gone through. I didn't know his father, but I never wanted to meet him. Tristan covered my hands with his and I realized my hands were trembling.

"You understand why I didn't want that to be known by everyone?"

I nodded. "How old were you?"

"Ten," Tristan said. "My father made us each go through the test when we were ten. I was the only one who had an affinity for second magic system. My father knows, Tiana knows, now you know. I've never told anyone else."

"Is that how the seventh son ended up as the ruler?" I asked.

"I'm not officially the ruler," he said. "But yes, it is how I ended up as the heir to my father's throne."

"Didn't your siblings ask questions?" I asked.

He shook his head. "You don't ask my father questions."

Considering Tristan's reputation, it was terrifying to consider that his father scared him. I lifted my hand, an overwhelming desire to touch his face, to be closer to him. I wanted to comfort him and tell him that everything was going to turn out fine.

He pulled away from me before I could touch him. "I'm trusting you with this. Both the Summer magic and the fact that I can share memories."

"Thank you for showing me," I said, lowering my hand. I ached to touch him, to be near him. But I knew that wasn't a good idea. Letting any of my lust for Tristan through would make things far too complicated. "I'll keep your secret."

I could understand why he didn't want people to find out that he could wield magic from two different kingdoms after I saw how strongly Tiana reacted toward me for having magic for more than one. Though, she didn't threaten him the way she threatened me. "Tiana doesn't know about your ability to share memories, does she? Is it because she never tested your winter magic?"

It was coming in sharper focus now, the fact that Tristan held secrets about his true strength from Tiana and everyone else. It was a weapon he could wield against any enemy that they'd never see coming. From a strategic point of view, it was brilliant.

Tristan nodded. "It's the only thing I have against her, in case I ever have a reason to challenge her."

"Do you think you will need to challenge her?" I asked.

"When you have a father like mine, you grow up with a target on your back. You learn to start collecting things on others. Things you can use against them if you ever need to," he said.

"What are you collecting about me?" The words came out before I thought through meaning.

He chuckled softly and a hint of a smile played at his lips. "I can't tell you that. You're smart enough to realize what your own weaknesses are."

"Why are you helping me?" I asked. "For real. This goes beyond the promise you made me. You promised you would help us to defeat the monsters and they're gone. Yet, you're not. Is this really about paying tribute to your late wife?"

"That's a good question for another time." Tristan cleared his throat. "Now you know what to expect in the test. What I just gave you is the closest you'll ever come to feeling it firsthand. Until your own test, that is. I don't think you're going to experience the same pain that I did because I do think you're going to test as having an affinity for every court. She'll likely to start with Summer, since that's the one we're least sure about. The way to complete each test the quickest is to find that point of your magic, the pinnacle, and set it free. Don't resist. When you feel it coming, let it go. Encourage it and don't hold back."

I stood and lifted my chin to make eye contact with Tristan. "Thank you. I'm sorry you had to go through that."

I wanted to ask about Sasha and his other siblings, but if I'd learned anything from Tristan, it was that he gave information freely when it was information he was willing to share. The fact that he hadn't offered to tell me about them, made me think he wasn't ready to share. It was similar to Cormac, but he didn't lock everything down for me, only I suspected, the really painful things.

My heart ached for him and I had an overwhelming urge to pull him into my embrace and whisper comforting words into his ear. But he wasn't Ethan and he wasn't Dane. Tristan was something else entirely and I didn't know exactly how to respond to him. All I knew was that with each passing moment the two of us spent together, I was growing more and more attached to the Winter Prince. I wanted to keep my distance from him, but he kept making it harder for me to do. He let me in, even when he didn't have to.

"You should eat. And try to relax, save your strength." Tristan walked to the doors and opened them. Ethan, true to his word, was waiting outside. The two males exchanged a glance as they passed.

"How did it go?" Ethan asked.

"Fine," I said. "I think I'll be ready when she tests me."

Ethan nodded, his tight lipped expression more serious than usual. "Good."

I took a deep breath in and let it out, telling myself I needed to let go of some of the tension I was holding. Tristan was right, there wasn't much more I could do to prepare. And if he was correct about me having magic from each of the four Courts, I didn't have anything to worry about when it came to receiving pain during the test. For some reason, that didn't make me feel better. I had a feeling that if Tiana found me to have all four Courts, I was in for a heap of trouble.

# Chapter Twenty-One

❦

When dinner was announced, I declined, stating that I wasn't hungry after the snacks that have been brought to the room on the fourth floor. Apparently, the dignitaries ate in a grand dining hall of some sort. I wasn't interested in spending any more time with Tiana than I had to. Two of Tristan's guards trailed behind me as I paced down the hall, trying to keep my head clear while I waited for my test. I knew I still had a bit of time before she came, but I couldn't bring myself to relax.

The House of the Moon was a strange place, half palace, half brothel. As I continued to walk, reflecting on the oddness of the combination, I couldn't help but wonder at how much of Tristan's past happened here or at places like it. I knew I shouldn't care, but every time we spoke, it seemed like we forged a deeper connection. It wasn't the same as what I felt with Ethan, but there was a connection there. I wondered if he felt it too. It made me feel guilty, like I was betraying the others, but it was hard to suppress.

I pressed my palms into my temples and tried to think of something else. The last thing I wanted to do when I met with Tiana, who could read my mind, was to be sitting there thinking about Tristan. I knew she'd find a way to use that against me if she knew that I was starting to develop strong feelings toward him. Deciding I needed a distraction, I walked down the stairs. Tristan's guards silently followed me, but didn't object to me leaving the fourth floor. Before I realized where I was going, I found myself in front of Laney's room. I hesitated, wondering if I should knock. It was possible she had a client and showing up outside her door could be seen as unprofessional.

Pressing my ear to the door, I listened for any sign of her or any visitors she might be entertaining. After a few heartbeats of not hearing anything, I knocked quietly on the door.

Laney opened the door, a wide grin on her face. "I wasn't sure if I'd see you again." She glanced at the guards behind me and her brow furrowed. "Your entourage?"

"Tristan, I mean His Grace insisted."

"Can she come in?" Lainey asked the guards behind me. "It's a pretty small room, I'm not sure all of us will fit, but you're all invited."

One of the guards peeked his head in the room and looked around. "Leave the door open."

"Thanks." Lainey grabbed my hand and tugged me into the room. "Come on, tell me all about how the meeting with the fancy dignitary went."

I shook my head. "I don't want to talk about that right now. I don't have much time. I just need a distraction, anything to help me clear my mind."

Lainey gave me a gentle push toward her pillows in the corner, her only real seating area unless we wanted to sit on the bed. I sat down tucking my feet under me. "I'm not taking away time from clients, am I?"

"Oh no," she said. "When we lose our clients, like you saw last night, we do get a little punishment. No clients for me for a week. So I have plenty of free time if you stick around," she said.

"I'm so sorry." I knew she was saving money and sending it

back to her family. A week without making anything was probably rough.

She shrugged and pulled a box out from under her bed. Walking over to me, she shrugged. "It's not so bad. I'm sure I'll make it up next week."

She settled onto the cushion next to me and set the box in between us. Lifting the lid she revealed what looked to be a game with lots of little pieces. "You said you need a distraction; this is my favorite game. I rarely have time to play, but this seems like the perfect time."

Lainey laid out a wooden board that she pieced together from the contents of the box then set up a series of game pieces across the squares. "Have you ever played?"

I shook my head. My father had a couple of games like this in his study, but he never permitted my sister or me to play them.

"You can be red and I'll be black. The object of the game is to capture the other's queen. Sound fun?" she asked.

"You might have to walk me through the first time," I said.

Laney explained what each piece could do and how to play the game as we each took turns going through the motions.

As I got the hang of the game, I started thinking ahead of just one or two moves. There was a lot of strategy and every detail had to be considered. Laney was an excellent opponent, keeping me guessing at every move.

While I played, there was no time to worry about anything else. I got completely sucked into the game and focused all of my attention on trying to capture Laney's queen. The time flew by, the first round ending horribly for me; the second round proving to be more of an evenly matched playing field.

A gentle knock sounded on the door and we both turned.

"I'm sorry, My Lady, but it's time," one of the guards said.

My shoulders sank and I looked longingly at the unfinished game in front of me. "I wish I could stay and finish."

"Me too. You know where to find me." Lainey gently swept the pieces off the board and into the box. Then she picked up the flat pieces that made up the board and stacked them together before sealing the whole thing back into its container.

There was something symbolic about watching her close the game box. I wouldn't be able to delay the test, the longer I sat there, the worse it would probably be for me.

With a sinking feeling in my gut, I forced myself to stand and gave Laney a weak smile. "I hope we'll see each other soon."

Lainey hugged me, catching me off guard, just for a moment. I smiled, embracing her back. I never would have guessed that after everything, while staying at a brothel, I'd make one of the first true friends in my new life. Possibly, one of the first true friends ever. The other children I played with growing up so easily walked away from me when my father threatened them. I didn't blame them, but something told me Laney wouldn't give up on a friend as easily. I let go of her and stepped away, heavy sadness hanging over me as I worried this might be the last time I saw her.

"We need to go now," a guard said.

I sighed and gave Lainey one last smile. "Thank you, for everything."

"I should be thanking you. If not for you last night, I don't really want to think about what that orc would have done to me."

I gave her one more, quick hug, then turned and left the room. My throat was tight as we parted. I hope she was going to be safe and I hoped I was going to survive. There were a lot of things about us that made us different, like she had said, there were a lot of things about us that were the same.

Silently, I followed the guards to the fourth floor. When we arrived, Tiana's guards were already stationed outside the double doors. One of them nodded as I approached and reached for the doorknob, opening the door for me.

I glanced around quickly, hoping to catch sight of one of my princes. A familiar face would go a long way toward soothing my nerves, but none of them were around.

My chest felt tight as I crossed the threshold into the large room. I knew this needed to be done, it was the only way to send Tiana back to where she came from and the only way to get the audience I so desperately needed with the Queen. I had to learn how to control this magic.

Tiana stood when I approached. She was in a new dress, still gold, but this time it was slimmer, hugging her figure. The plunging neckline and generous slit up the side left little to the imagination. Every inch of it was covered in thousands of shimmering gems. The dress barely skimmed the floor whereas her last one left the puddle of fabric in her wake. I supposed this dress was the formal attire she changed into for dinner. I tried not to think about her slinking around my princes in something so obviously designed to show off her body. It made me hate her even more.

"Are you ready?" Tiana asked.

No formality, straight to business. I nodded. "I'm ready."

Tiana gestured to one of the chairs and I followed the silent order, settling into the seat.

Tiana snapped her fingers and one of the guards came bolting into the room. A moment of panic welled up inside me as the large male Fae in the burgundy and gold uniform trotted over to me.

Before I could get too nervous, he picked up the chair that was across from me and moved it next to me. With a bow, he took his leave, closing the door behind him.

Tiana settled into the chair next to me and extended her hands, palms up, just as she had done in the memory I'd seen. I hesitated, wondering if I should wait for an order.

"Go ahead, I know Tristan told you what you have to do." Her voice was surprisingly gentle, as if pretending to be kind. That sent a chill through me straight to my bones.

I tightened my jaw, then lifted my hands and slowly moved them over to Tiana's waiting palms. Her hands were like ice and I almost pulled away on instinct from the sheer surprise of how cool they were. Instead, I managed to force my hands to stay, as steady as I could, waiting for her to begin.

# Chapter Twenty-Two

✦❖✦

I braced myself, as green strands of shimmering lights wound their way around my hands. Tiana wasn't wasting any time getting started and as Tristan anticipated, she started with Summer.

I waited for the pain to come and took a deep breath, trying to center myself. I had no idea what kind of magic I had inside of me and I didn't know how to fully control it. Tristan had said that if I had an affinity for the type of magic I was being tested for, I should let the magic go in the same way I had practiced finding it when I worked with Cormac.

Tiana's eyes were locked on me and I knew she was studying me. I didn't want to drag this out any longer than necessary. I closed my eyes, letting my thoughts wander through my body, paying attention to every flicker and every movement. If I had magic from the Summer Court, I wanted to show a sign of it so we could be finished here.

All at once, I felt it. That familiar clawing sensation only this time it burned. I winced as tongues of flame seemed to lap at my insides. Was this the pain that came from not having the power or was this my magic responding to the test?

I took a deep breath again and focused on seeing if I could find the origin point for what I was feeling. Mentally searching, I managed to find a thread that felt like it could be the pinnacle of the magic I was looking for.

Using what I had learned from Cormac, I tugged on the thread, eager to get it to respond to me. Another surge of heat rose through me and I gritted my teeth, letting out a grunt. I opened my eyes and stared at Tiana. She was smiling at me, and I wondered if she thought my response was caused by a lack of magic. I knew for sure that wasn't the case. I maintained eye contact with her as I continued to pull on the thread, willing the magic to surface.

As far as I knew, I had never called on this magic before. It felt foreign and uncomfortable, but the more I focused, the more it responded. Another rush of heat surged through me and my hands trembled. Trying to capitalize on the surge, I directed it as best I could through me, into my hands, and into Tiana. I wanted to burn that smirk right off her face.

Tiana's eyes widened, then she looked down. I followed her gaze and felt a swell of triumph as I watched the green bindings start to gain in intensity as the green shifted to yellow, then gold, and finally bright orange as flames danced in a circle around our hands.

Tiana broke contact, tearing her hands away from me. The smile was gone from her face now.

"You do have Summer magic." She wiped her palms on her dress then extended them again, slower this time, as if some of her confidence had seeped out.

I didn't say anything, I simply set my hands on top of hers once more.

This time, shimmery silver strands wrapped around our hands. I knew she was testing me for the Winter Court. As the threads tightened around our hands, pain shot through me. It was as if the clawing inside me was trying to turn me inside out.

I gasped against the sudden rise of intensity as magic wreathed and twisted and turned inside me. I'd never felt a response like this before. Suddenly, I was standing inside a stable. Quiet conversation sounded near me and I turned, surprised to see Tiana with Cormac. Tiana had tears streaming down her face, Cormac was just as serious as ever.

"How long have we been friends, Cormac?" Tina said.

"I'm still your friend, but you don't understand the pressure I'm under. I can't endorse a different candidate than my father. You know what he would do to me."

"You can't do this to me." She wiped the tears from her face. "I need this, Cormac. This is my one shot."

"I'm sorry, I've already cast my ballot. I can't change it now."

Tiana scowled. "You're weak, you know that?"

"Tiana, some people just aren't meant to be Queen. Your sister, she's a natural born diplomat. She knows how to handle herself."

"And I don't?" Tiana asked. "I thought this was about your father. Since when do you care who wins the title of Queen?"

"Tiana, I can't support you for this."

"You owe me, Cormac," she said. "You know that."

"You do realize that being sister of the Queen is a very strong place of power," Cormac said.

"And you realize," Tiana said. "That if I don't get this endorsement over my sister, I'm going to be putting pressure on Angela."

"You can do whatever you want, she's already declined. She knows she's not cut out for it."

"I have more power than you think. Change your vote." The tears were gone from Tiana's face now her gaze on Cormac was like fire or maybe ice. She was doing everything she could to try and manipulate him.

A sting hit my cheek as someone's palm came in contact with my face. I gasped and opened my eyes to find Tiana hovering in front of me, hand drawn back ready to hit me again. "That wasn't for you."

"I don't even know what happened," I said.

"Who sent you?" she asked.

"No one, I swear. I don't even know how that happened. I don't know what I did and I wouldn't be able to repeat it even if I wanted to."

Tiana narrowed her eyes and lowered her hand. Jaw tight, she stared at me, unblinking. Finally, she backed away from me and settled into her chair. "You will never speak of what you just saw to anyone. All parts of what happens in a test is confidential. If I hear that you broke that confidentiality, I'll have you tried for treason."

I swallowed and nodded. "I won't tell anyone. I'm not here for any reason, that I can tell you. I'm just here because I want to figure out how to survive. Cormac told me the creatures from the Under are attracted to untamed magic and he mentioned that if I couldn't control it, it was possible I could be in even greater danger. I just want to learn how to tame this and live in peace."

Tiana narrowed her eyes and crossed her arms over her chest. "You're very convincing, I almost believe you."

"I'm serious. I have no greater ambition than that."

"If that were true, why would all the princes be helping you? And why did you reappear just in time for Queen's Trial?" she asked.

"They're helping me because they're the ones who found me. I can't explain the timing. I just want to have a meeting with the Queen."

"Let's finish this then," Tiana said, extending her hands in front of me again.

Dread hung heavy in the pit of my stomach as I slowly set my hands on top of hers. Terrified of what would happen next, I swallowed down the fear as pink shimmering threads wrapped their way around my hands.

The magic inside felt a bit weaker this time, but it was still there. This time, I understood why Cormac had insisted on the importance of keeping the magic near the surface at all times. It would be much easier if I learned how to keep the magic with me so I could use it when needed.

Thinking of what Cormac had said about clearing my mind, I focused on finding the pinnacle. It came quicker than last time, even if it was weaker. I harnessed what I could of the feeling, forcing it into my hands as I had done before.

To my surprise, the pink strands changed before my eyes into little pink flower buds. My eyes widened as the flowers opened and I couldn't help but smile at how something so beautiful had come out of thin air. Tiana pulled her hands away snapping the vines that had replaced the pink strands. The little flowers fell to the floor.

"That's three." Tiana extended her hands again, not making a scene out of the fact that I had magic from the Spring Court. That left us with Autumn, the final court.

I set my hands in Tiana's and braced myself.

The gold strands wrapped around my hands sending a rush of power through me I didn't recognize. This wasn't a clawing. This was like a wave rolling through me. Every part of my skin tingled with a level of awareness unlike anything I'd ever experienced. My pulse raced as my breathing grew rapid. Whatever was happening wasn't what I expected. There was no pain, but the sensations I was experiencing were overwhelming. As if I was feeling the dust floating in the air as it passed over my skin.

I watched the gold strands, waiting for them to do something in response to the power surging through me. I'd seen them catch on fire and grow plants, but I couldn't even guess what they'd do with Autumn magic. Suddenly, I could no longer see my hands. Only Tiana's surrounded by the glowing threads. There was still a space where my hands should be, but I couldn't see them.

Tiana dropped her hands, breaking the connection and as

soon as she did, my hands reappeared. I held them up in front of me, inspecting them. "What was that?"

"It seems you are able to take stealth to a whole new level," Tiana said. "I've heard rumors of hunters who can make themselves invisible, but I thought they were only rumors."

"I can turn invisible?" I asked.

"Well, with the aid of the test you can. It doesn't mean you will be able to harness that in real life." She frowned.

I tested as having magic for each of the four Courts. Just as the princes had predicted. What did that mean for me moving forward? "Can I see the queen now?"

Tiana frowned. "I thought Cormac was testing me. I never thought you actually had the magic of all four Courts."

"Please," I said, nearly begging. "I need help with this. I don't want to be monster food and I don't want to draw monsters to those I care about."

She raised an eyebrow. "All four of them, right?"

My heart pounded. I had a feeling the more she knew about me, the more fuel I gave her against me in the future. Something was telling me to protect myself with her. I knew I needed to be careful with my words. "Of course, I care about all of them. They've helped me. And as you said, had I met you, you'd have thrown me to the beasts."

"This changes things you know." She stood, the fight seeming to have gone from her.

"What do you mean?" I asked.

"We have to see the Queen immediately." She walked toward the door, not looking back at me.

I scurried behind her. "Are we going now?"

"Try to keep up," she said without turning around.

The doors opened as she approached and she swept through, I stayed behind her. I didn't want to be depending on Tiana for anything. Least of all my meeting with the Queen, but I knew I needed to see her.

"How did it go?" Dane asked, hurrying to catch up with us as we walked down the hall.

"I'm not sure," I said, which was the truth. I now knew I had the powers of all four Courts, but I didn't know what that meant. Tiana's reaction wasn't exactly as I'd hoped.

"Where are we going?" Dane asked.

"You are going nowhere," Tiana said. "But you can fetch Cormac. I don't want you anywhere near me."

Dane looked like he wanted to object, but he held his tongue.

"We'll be in the lobby," Tiana said. "Hurry back, errand boy."

My brow furrowed and my jaw tightened at the words Tiana used toward Dane. She had no reason to be so terrible to people. Then, I remembered that Dane and she had a past. It wasn't my business and it was possible that she had a right to be upset. Especially if he had gone to bed her and then turned her down before the test. I really hoped that wasn't the case, but I wasn't sure what had happened in the brief time they were away from me today.

I could hear Tiana's guards following behind us, staying with us as we made our way back down to the main floor. At the bottom of the staircase, Tiana stopped and I looked up from the ground to see Tristan blocking her descent.

"Move," Tiana said. "I have no quarrel with you, Winter Prince."

"You will if you take my guest without my consent," he said.

"I'm taking her to see my sister," Tiana said. "Isn't that what you wanted?"

"It is, but I know you far too well to let you take her alone. I'll be accompanying you," Tristan said.

A surge of gratitude welled up inside me at Tristan's insistence that he attend the meeting with the Queen. While meeting the Queen was exactly what I wanted, going anywhere with Tiana was not on my list of things to do.

"You're not welcome in Faerie, you know that, Tristan," Tiana said.

"My father is not welcome," he said.

"I'll vouch for him," Cormac said as he walked down the hall toward us. Ethan and Dane were right behind him.

My heart leaped at the sight of all my princes in the same place at the same time. I felt safe with any one of them, but safest when they were all with me. I knew Tiana wasn't a danger to me while they were around.

"Fine, then," she said. "Try to keep up."

Tiana grabbed my wrist, squeezing so hard her fingernails bit into my flesh. I tugged my arm away from her, but she kept hold tightly. Before I had a chance to open my mouth to protest, everything went black.

# Chapter Twenty-Three

I sucked in a breath but found no air to pull into my lungs. I was in a vacuum, cut off from the world around me. After a moment of panic, I realized Tiana must have grabbed me so we could slide. That didn't make the darkness around me any easier to handle.

A heartbeat later, I felt my feet touch down on solid ground seconds before my vision cleared. Breathing heavy, I glared at Tiana, then pulled my wrist away from her. She looked pleased with herself and I didn't feel like yelling at her. It would just let her know she succeeded in getting under my skin.

I looked around, trying to assess where we were. All around me were trees with orange leaves that formed a canopy, nearly blocking out the sun. Leaves crunched under my boots as I spun in a slow circle looking for any signs of life. As far as I could see, it was only Tiana and me. She'd taken me somewhere in the Autumn Court, but we weren't at the Queen's palace. "Where are we?"

"Near an entrance to the Under," she said. "I'm curious about your untamed magic. And you aren't meant to be alive. I'm going to let the monsters do what they should have done already."

My magic spiked inside me, sending a surge of tingles from my chest down into my arms. I didn't know what that meant or how to respond to it. In the past, it felt like a fight to let it out, but now, my magic seemed to be simmering below the surface. Instead of clawing, it was vibrating through me, soothing me.

"You don't want to do this," I said. "If those creatures get out, it won't just be me they take."

"So noble." She scoffed. "You really are just like her."

"Just like who?" I asked.

"My sister," she said. "You two might even get along. It's a shame she'll never meet you. But then again, if she wanted you to survive, she'd have told me about you."

My magic pulsed and throbbed, making me wince against its demands under my skin. I knew it wanted out, but I didn't know what it would do. Creating a blinding white light wasn't going to do me any good in the middle of a grove of trees. Where would I run? I'd be just as likely to injure myself as I was to escape. And maybe that was her plan all along. "I don't understand what you're saying. Please, you said you'd take me to the Queen. You said you'd help me."

"She told me you were taken care of. She told me she had you killed," Tiana said.

"Who?" I asked, my magic flailing with my temper. The more Tiana babbled nonsense without giving me any information, the more upset I was feeling. Part of me wanted to unleash this on her, but I wasn't like her. I didn't want to hurt anyone even if she might deserve it.

"The Queen isn't supposed to have children because they turn out like you. Born with all four Courts worth of magic. It's forbidden. Nobody but the Queen herself can have that much magic. She won't even let me know where the key to the temple is. And yet, here you are. You did nothing to earn the magic flowing through your veins." Tiana's words came out like a curse. "You should be dead."

I nearly stumbled backward at Tiana's confession. How was this possible? I couldn't be the daughter of a Queen, could I?

"She lied to me," Tiana said. "Imagine how she'll feel when I tell her of your untimely end."

The magic flared like an explosion inside me, knocking me to the ground. There was no blinding light this time, just me in the dirt. I pushed myself to sitting and brushed the dirt and dried leaves off of my hands. I could hear Tiana cackling in front of me, but my hair had fallen in front of my eyes. Tossing my head, I used my forearm to move the curls away.

It wasn't just Tiana in front of me. Behind her, stalking in with the stealth and grace of a cat were four creatures that looked like walking nightmares. Their front legs were lean and covered in black fur, their faces were that of large birds. Feathers and beady eyes and sharp, pointed beaks. Large wings were folded along their smooth feline bodies.

I scrambled to my feet and backed away. Each of the four beasts faces turned toward me, focusing their beady little eyes on me. One of them snapped its beak and let out a screech that made me wince.

Tiana didn't seem bothered by the creatures. In fact, the creatures didn't seem bothered by her, either. They walked around her, ignoring her, in favor of me. Was it the magic they were drawn to? "What are those things?"

"These sweet creatures?" Tiana purred.

I knew they weren't sweet. They smelled of the decay I'd caught so often on the Sodalis and was filling my nostrils. These creatures were monsters capable of murder. And I was likely their current target.

"These are my griffins," Tiana said. "I lured them here from the Under after my sister won the crown. They do my bidding and mine alone."

I continued to take slow backward steps, careful of where I

set my feet. Falling in a hole or twisting my ankle could be the end of me. "Tiana, don't do this. I mean you no harm."

"Liar."

"Honestly," I said. "I didn't even know about Faerie until a few days ago. I didn't even know I was Fae. I thought I was human. Someone was paying them to keep me in the human realm, honest," I said.

"And now we know who that was," she said, inching closer to me. Her beasts moving alongside her. "My sister told me she had you killed. That was her punishment for violating our laws and having a child as Queen. She lied to me. And now I will make you both pay."

I needed a way out of here. There was nothing I was going to say that would cause Tiana to let me go. The problem was, if I escaped, where would I go? She'd taken me away from the Winter Court to a place that was unfamiliar to me. I didn't have the ability to slide. All I could do was run.

"If you're going to run, you better do it now. They haven't eaten in a few days and as loyal as they are, I'm not sure how much longer they'll wait before they devour you."

That was all I needed to hear. I turned and gathered up the fabric of my dress as I ran, holding it in a ball against my waist with one arm while I pumped the other to gain as much speed as I could. Behind me, the sound of the beasts running through the woods echoed like a countdown to my demise. Every crunching leaf, every slap of a branch, even the beating of my own heart were like a symphony of destruction. It was a matter of time before the creatures caught me.

I flew through the trees, over roots and rocks, under low hanging branches. Should I try to climb a tree? No, the beasts had wings. Why did everything from the Under have wings?

Could I blind them with magic? Would that help? My heart sank. They were predators. They'd smell me even if they couldn't see me.

My chest burned and a sharp pain shot through my side. I wasn't sure how much longer I could outrun the griffins. I needed help.

As I ran, the sounds of the creatures grew softer and more subdued. There were still snarling noises and sounds of movement, but it was fading. I risked a backward glance and saw that the griffins had turned away from me, racing back to the place where I had left Tiana.

Had they turned on her? That didn't make any sense. The magic I had was supposed to attract them not send them away. Not that I was complaining, but it was confusing. A flicker of something pulled me back toward the sounds of the snarls and growls of the griffins.

Ignoring the part of me that wanted to flee, I turned back, straining to see what was happening with the monsters. The closer I got, the louder the shrieks of the creatures grew. Finally, I got close enough to make out what they were doing. My heart sank.

They weren't attacking Tiana, they were in the middle of a battle. The princes must have found me and I wasn't about to let them fight this on their own. Especially not since I was the one who caused all this trouble in the first place.

I picked up my pace, still holding my dress in a ball of fabric on my waist. As I got closer, I saw Ethan wrestling one of the griffins while Tristan removed a knife from a fallen beast. Cormac had Tiana on the ground, pinning her in place with his knee. Dane actually looked like he was having a good time fighting two of the beasts at once.

I took a step toward Dane, thinking he was the one most likely in need of help since he was outnumbered, then I doubled back, turning toward Ethan. The memory Tiana brought back to me so recently was too fresh in my mind to walk away from Ethan in the battle. What if he was still recovering from his injury? I knew my healing magic wasn't as strong as his and I wasn't sure what kind of a fix I had actually done for him.

As I charged toward Ethan, he landed a kick on the side of the beast, making it screech before it turned and snapped its jaws at Ethan's face. He jumped out of the way, dodging the sharp beak. He didn't have any weapons and he wasn't using magic that I could see. As I got closer, though, my own magic flared, as if being directed by someone else. I wondered if I was reacting to him.

Ethan caught my eye as I stood just outside the creature's reach. "Wings," Ethan shouted.

I didn't hesitate, I jumped up on top of the creature grabbed its wings, pinning them to the feline body underneath. The creature shrieked again, and fell to its side, knocking me to the ground. I held on, wrapping my legs around the beast to keep the wings pinned. I struggled to maintain my hold as the griffin rolled around, trying to break free of my grip.

The haunches and back of the beast were strong and as it struggled, the muscles flexed underneath of me. I wasn't sure how I was keeping it down, but I knew it had to do with the wings.

The griffin rolled, and my back scraped against the rocks and dirt of the ground. I winced as my head scraped along a bush, sending a fresh wave of pain as it sliced into my cheek.

I held on, catching glimpses of Ethan in front of the creature's face, too close to the sharp beak for my comfort. I couldn't tell what he was doing, but I wanted to help him. A moment later the creature convulsed under me then remained still. Breathing heavy, I let go and looked up to see Ethan, covered in Griffin blood. He held a small knife in his hand and his usually sparkling eyes looked dull and glassy.

Silently, he extended a hand for me, and I took it, allowing him to pull me up. The once beautiful dress was now covered in dirt and I did my best to brush the large chunks off of me before balling it back up into a pile at my waist so I could move more freely. Then, I looked around for the next place that I could be of assistance only to realize that it was very quiet. The only sound came from the grunts and protests of Tiana in Cormac's grip.

# Chapter Twenty-Four

"I s now the proper time to skip protocol and go right to see the Queen?" Tristan asked. His hands were covered in blood and his white tunic was ruined. But he didn't seem to notice.

"You will remove your hands from me now, *Your Grace*," Tiana said, emphasizing Cormac's title.

"You tried to kill an innocent," Cormac said.

"The griffins came out of the tear in the Under. It could have happened to anyone," Tiana said.

"You're a liar," I yelled. "You told me you brought me here to kill me."

"Your girl has a vivid imagination," Tiana said. "I brought her here for the final test to ensure that my findings were accurate. This is a sacred space, after all, and you all know the magic is stronger here than it is indoors."

As if on cue, a gust of wind blew through the trees, shaking the leaves. It sent a shiver through me and for an instant, I questioned my own memory of the event. Shaking my head, I squared my shoulders. "She's lying. She said I was supposed to be dead already. She said the Queen is my mother."

"That's not possible, Love," Dane said. "The Queen can't have children."

"That's not true," Cormac said. "The Queen isn't *allowed* to have children. It's not that she can't, technically. And it would explain Cassia's magic."

"And the money being paid to keep you in the mortal realm," Ethan said.

"What does that make her?" Dane asked. "A princess?"

My cheeks heated as I turned away from Tristan's smirk. Had he known the whole time?

"No," Ethan said. "It doesn't work that way. Cassia's right, she technically isn't supposed to exist." Ethan squeezed my hand in his. "But I'm glad she does."

"Are you three going to spend the next hour professing your love for this illegal Fae while there's an open tear to the Under?"

Cormac straightened, still holding Tiana. Then, he yanked her up to standing.

She squealed. "Careful, lover, I remember what foreplay was with you."

I tightened my grip on Ethan's hands and my fingernails bit into my palm on my other hand. There was no way Cormac would fall for this female. She was pure evil. And to insinuate that she'd been intimate with him sent rage burning through me.

"I made her jealous," Tiana said, wrinkling her nose. "Isn't that cute? She's already had two of you, but the greedy girl wants you all."

I pursed my lips, staring daggers at Tiana.

"Oops, was I supposed to keep my mouth shut about the things I saw in your mind?"

"That's enough," Dane said, walking over to her. He grabbed her other arm. "Show us where the tear is. Then we'll take you to the Queen. She can figure out what to do with you."

"I'll stay with Cassia," Tristan said.

"Wait, Cormac," Ethan said. "I'll go. You're the one who can get to the Queen. She'll listen to *you*."

Cormac seemed to ponder Ethan's words for a moment and then he nodded. "I'll Take Tiana with us. You and Dane find the tear and seal it. Tristan?" Cormac looked over at the Winter Prince.

"Are you inviting me for a visit with the Queen?" Tristan asked.

"Are you willing to help or not?" Cormac asked.

Tristan walked over to where Dane and Cormac were holding Tiana between them. He grabbed hold of her arm just above where Dane was holding. "I'll take it from here."

Tiana's expression was smug as she was passed off from Dane to Tristan. I scowled at her and wondered what she was thinking. She was too quiet and it made me nervous. The sooner we could get her to the Queen and turn her over for what she did, the better.

Cormac extended his hand to me. "Come, Cassia. It's time to slide."

I grabbed Cormac's hand while trying to keep my distance from Tiana. I wasn't thrilled about sliding through the void with Cormac while he held Tiana's hand. I wanted to get to the Queen and this was the fastest way possible. After days of traveling, I now really wished we had skipped the travel through the Winter Court and gone straight to the Queen.

While the delay had revealed Tristan's true colors, which were surprisingly supportive, it had resulted in the meeting and tests from Tiana. I couldn't help but wonder what would have happened if we'd gone straight to the Queen. Would she have turned us away? Would she still have asked her sister to test me? My stomach clenched at the thought of meeting this person who was a stranger to me, yet according to Tiana, wasn't truly a stranger. If Tiana was correct, she was my mother by birth.

*Mother.* The word felt strange and uncomfortable in my head as I rolled it around my thoughts, trying to get a feel for it. The human woman who raised me still came to mind when I thought of the word *mother*. The Queen was a stranger and if what everyone said was correct, she wasn't supposed to have children. How would she react to meeting the child she tried to hide in the human world?

"Hold on tight," Cormac said, his words breaking my thoughts.

I squeezed his hand harder, bracing myself for the darkness that was about to swallow me as we slid to the Queen's Palace. I took a deep breath and all too soon it was cut short, as the void closed in around me, sending me into nothingness as we entered into the slide.

Usually, I felt like I was hovering in place, unable to focus on the sensations around me. But something felt wrong the second everything went black. I felt like I was being pulled and pushed and dragged in multiple directions at once. Gasping, I tried to find balance that wouldn't come. I felt like I was spinning out of control. I reached out with my free hand trying to feel Cormac next to me, but there was nothing. His hand wasn't even in mine anymore.

Panic surged through me as I kicked and fought against the suffocating darkness. Suddenly, light returned, and I shielded my eyes from the surprising brightness of it. Then, I landed hard on the ground twisted on my side, in a pile of dirt. I rubbed my eyes, staring into the bright sunlight gasping for breath. I didn't recognize where I was. The only thing I knew was that I was alone.

I pushed myself to standing and brushed the pebbles and dirt from my palms as I looked around. From the looks of it, still in the Autumn Court. Orange trees that reminded me of the grove we had just left grew in the distance.

Around me were tall grasses, yellow and faded, which swayed in the breeze. Quickly, I found the sun and wondered why I hadn't paid much attention to where it was last time I'd been lost here. Should I head for the trees? It was possible it was the same trees that I just left behind. Which might mean that Ethan and Cormac were there, trying to seal the tear between this world and the Under. But then again, would I be putting them at risk if I took my untamed magic so near a tear to the Under? I didn't want to attract anything that might spring forth and harm them.

I spun a slow circle, looking for any sign of life. What happened? Did Cormac let go of me? That didn't seem possible. Cormac would never let go of me. It had to be Tiana. She must've done something while we were sliding.

If that was the case, I knew Tristan and Cormac would be looking for me. I also knew that Ethan had a way of finding me no matter where I went. The thought was comforting, but I wasn't ready for him to find me yet. I wanted him to be able to finish taking care of that tear so no other awful monsters could find their way into these lands.

Hoping he could sense how I was feeling, I cleared my head, focusing on the fact that at least right now, I was safe. Nothing was chasing me, no one was trying to kill me, I wasn't even at risk from the elements right then. If anything, this was the least danger I had been in practically since arriving in Faerie.

I squinted into the horizon, completing one more small circle before I decided which direction to walk. Opposite the grove of trees, I could just make out the lines of what looked to be a road. Roads meant the possibility of civilization. I might be able to ask someone for directions on how to reach the palace. I knew it was risky to hope I'd run into someone after the attack at the Winter Court, but I had to hope that most of the Fae didn't know who I was or what I looked like. Add in the fact that I was no longer traveling with an entourage of princes and my ruined clothes made me look more peasant than princess. I cringed at the word. I knew it wasn't an accurate description of what I was by birth, but the pet name from Tristan was closer to the truth than I had imagined.

Steeling myself, I walked toward the road. *Ethan, whenever you're done, please come find me.* With any luck, he'd find me before I ran into anyone who would harm me.

Hoping there were more good Fae in Faerie than bad, I walked toward the road.

# Chapter Twenty-Five

L ike most of my travels through Faerie so far, the road was
occupied by nobody but me. The pressed dirt road was well
groomed, another sure sign that I was in Autumn Court. Now
that I had reached the road, I had another decision to make. It
stretched out as far as I could see in both directions. Neither
giving me a clear indicator of which route I should take. I
watched as the wind blew through the tall grass sending it
rippling across the fields. The scent of wood smoke carried
through the air and I turned toward it as a flicker of recognition
flashed through me. Smoke was a good sign of civilization. Or at
least a cottage burning a fire. If for some reason, Ethan couldn't
find me before nightfall, I would need shelter. While I knew we
weren't in the Winter Court, It would likely get very cold after
the sunset.

I dropped the bundled fabric of my skirt that I had been
holding as I walked through the tall grasses. Now that I was on a
road, I felt like I'd have a better chance of convincing someone to
help me if I looked like a girl from some money who lost her way.
I laughed to myself as I considered how true that likely was now.

If I was the daughter of a Queen, it was possible I could ask her to pay someone for helping me. But first, I'd have to find help.

I wondered how far I'd have to walk before I found someone who could help or before someone found me. How long did it take to seal a tear to the Under? And where had Cormac, Tiana, and Tristan gone? I tensed at the thought of Tiana. I hadn't stopped to consider the fact that if she was nearby, she might try to harm me again.

I looked behind me, nervous at being so exposed in the open. My only other option was to hide in the grass or run toward the woods and wait for someone to rescue me. I really didn't want to be the 'wait to be rescued' type. I had a feeling waiting would be more dangerous than moving.

Cormac told me to follow my instincts so that was what I was doing. A sinking feeling in my gut told me I was at risk no matter what choice I made. That's how it had been since I arrived here. I'd been on the run from monsters and now I had the angry sister of the Queen, my apparent birth mother, trying to finish me off. If it weren't for meeting the princes and finding absolute joy in their company, I would take my chances back in the human realm.

The fancy slippers I'd been given to wear didn't protect my feet the way the boots I'd been wearing had. I felt every pebble and every stick and every uneven patch of ground as I walked. The next time I got dressed up, I was keeping the boots. Looking down so I could see where I stepped, I avoided pebbles and loose rocks that were in my way. I glanced back up, trying to keep my eyes fixed on the source of whatever was burning while also paying attention to where my feet were going to land.

So far, the smoke didn't appear to be getting any nearer. It might be farther away than I suspected. With a sigh, I continued walking, loneliness sinking in. I hoped I'd be reunited with the others soon. This time, I didn't have a doubt that we would meet again. This time, I knew they were looking for me. Last time I had been separated from the princes, I had just met them, I didn't know if they would spend their time searching for a stranger. We weren't strangers anymore. I knew they were a part of me and I was a part of them. There was something that told me the times we would be away from each other would be far fewer than the times we would be together.

The smell hit first, sending a chill straight down my spine. I would know that smell anywhere, the scent of death. I hadn't heard the creature approach, but I knew when I turned around I was going to see the monster. Clenching my hands into fists I braced myself for a fight. Slowly, I turned around and the fear that had been a trickle turned into an explosion, setting every nerve on fire as a scream got caught in my throat. This wasn't just one monster, at least a dozen giant, overgrown hairy bat creatures were snarling at me. Against one, I felt confident that I had a chance. What could I do against this many?

My magic clawed at my insides, sending pinpricks across my skin. It was flaring in a way I hadn't felt until the tests with Tiana and I wondered if she managed to unlock something that I hadn't tapped into yet.

Even with magic charging through me, I didn't know how to use it. But if I didn't do something, I was going to end up in a shredded pile of skin and bones after the monsters picked me clean. Reaching inside, I used every bit of my inner strength to unleash the part of me that wanted out. A booming sound echoed through the emptiness as the blinding white light I'd grown so familiar to seeing filled my view. Dazed, ears ringing, and terrified, I turned to where I hoped was the opposite direction of the creatures and I ran.

My heart thundered against my ribs, my breathing was strained, my arms and legs burned in protest against the tireless exertion of pushing myself to run faster than I ever had. I had to get somewhere where I could hide from these creatures or find someone who could help me fight them. Even with a weapon, even with being able to control my magic, I wasn't sure I'd stand a chance against this many beasts alone.

The edges of my vision blurred as I struggled to see through the white light. I wasn't sure if the light was fading for me or if my eyes were adjusting, but I knew I was running out of time. Trusting only my instincts I continued to run forward, losing both of my shoes in the process, but pressing on anyway.

My feet had taken quite a beating over the last several days and they still weren't healed fully, but there wasn't time to think about the pain in my feet. I just wanted to live.

Gasping for breath, I kept running even as I stumbled over my skirts. I picked myself back up off the ground and continued forward. By now, the light was fading and I could hear the snarls and roars of the creatures as they clambered forward, following my scent. My eyes darted around, searching for any sign of hope, anything that could help me.

*Ethan, if you can hear this, I need you.* Mentally calling out to him was a move of desperation, but I was out of ideas. In front of me I could hear noises as if a large group was moving in my direction. My chest tightened and I worried that I got turned around, and somehow was running straight into the monsters instead of away from them.

I turned and ran away from the sound, hoping I was cutting through the field instead of sticking to the road. Then something inside me told me to look back. I ignored it, but the thought wouldn't leave. Slowing down, I risked a backward glance at the fading white light to see a group of what looked like soldiers or guards making their way toward the Sodalis.

I stopped and fell to my knees as the guards intercepted the beasts, weapons extended in front of them. Tears streamed down my face as relief flooded through me. I didn't know who these guards were or why they had come, but I knew I would be monster food right now without them.

Exhausted, and emotionally drained, I watched, feeling helpless and hating every second of the feeling. Part of me longed to jump into the fight, but the guards were practiced with their swords and were eliminating the monsters efficiently. If I jumped in, I'd be an unarmed distraction, someone they'd have to protect or watch out for. It was possible I was likely to be more of a risk by jumping in than by staying back.

Again, the desire to learn how to use my magic and the desire to fight was rekindled. I didn't like the feeling of helplessness I was forced to hold onto as I watched these male and female Fae guards attack the monsters.

Where had they come from? Why were they here? I studied them as they parried and dodged and sliced the creatures with expert level precision. I narrowed my eyes, studying them. Their tunics were burgundy and they wore leather armor over their chests with a gold painted insignia I didn't recognize. All of them wore tan trousers and tall black leather boots.

They reminded me of the guards that had attended Tiana. My pulse, which I just recently begun to settle, climbed again. If these were her guards, were they here to capture me? Would they turn on me as soon as they dispatched the creatures?

I wiped the tear streaks off my cheeks and squared my jaw as I stood. I wasn't going to stand there and let them take me. They were distracted right now so this was my only chance. With a backward glance at the fight, I took off running through the field, hoping to find somewhere I could hide before they finished with the creatures.

The field seemed to expand forever around me, reminding me of the space we'd passed into before going into the Winter Court. As I raced through the grass, I scanned the scene looking for anywhere I might be able to hide.

"You, stop!" a voice called after me.

I didn't stop. I didn't even turn around. Tiana had already tried to kill me once and she was out there somewhere. It was possible she'd even sent these guards after me.

"Stop," the voice called again.

I ran harder.

Until I slammed into something and fell back onto the ground. Spots danced in front of my vision and my head throbbed from where I'd smacked the ground. The world spun as I sat up. Looking ahead of me, I could find no sign of what I'd run into. There was nothing there.

Frustrated and feeling like maybe I was losing my mind, I stood and extended my hand out in front of me. Despite the fact that it looked like nothing in front of me, there was a wall I couldn't see preventing entry. My heart felt like it fell from my chest as I realized I must be at an entrance to the Winter Court. And I was locked out.

# Chapter Twenty-Six

❧

When the guards grabbed me, I didn't even resist. The fight was gone and for the first time since I arrived here, I felt defeated. I'd been able to pass into the Winter Court before. Why would it change now?

I kept my gaze down as the guards on either side of me guided me back to the road. I wasn't even sure how many of them there were. All I knew was that there wasn't much hope for me to escape them.

My feet dragged as I followed them. Ethan hadn't come for me. Nobody had come for me. Exhaustion seemed to be seeping into my bones as hope faded. Whatever these guards wanted from me, they were going to get it. My willpower felt like it had been stripped from me, leaving me an empty shell of someone who once had goals and hopes and dreams. Now, I was just a changeling who was at the mercy of this group of Fae.

"Hurry up," one of the guards said as he tugged on my arm.

I glanced up at him, but hardly even registered what he looked like. All the guards seemed to be blending into a blur of burgundy and gold. My vision felt like it was swimming with color and I was struggling to focus on anything around me.

"Ease up," someone said. "You're going to kill her at this rate. The Queen wants her alive."

The mention of the Queen sent a pang through me that cut through the hazy feeling. I stopped walking and turned to the guard on my right. "We're going to the Queen?"

His brow furrowed. "Where else would the Queen's guard take you?"

"Where are we?" I asked.

He shook his head and tugged my arm, forcing me forward.

Feeling more alert than I had since hitting the invisible wall, I looked around and noticed that we weren't headed for the road. We were trudging through the tall grass. Ahead, I saw a large black gate standing in the middle of the tall grass. Had that always been there or had it just appeared? There was nothing else around. I would have noticed a gate in the middle of a field.

As we drew nearer to the gate, some of the guards ran ahead and to my surprise, the gate began to open.

"Are we at the palace?" I asked, already knowing the answer. The invisible wall I'd encountered hadn't been an entry to the Winter Court, it was a barrier hiding the Queen's Palace. Cormac's insistence that we approach the palace and seek a formal invitation made a bit more sense now. I wasn't even sure how you'd find the entrance if you weren't invited.

As the guards half pushed me through the opening, I wondered if I'd been dropped here on purpose. If Tiana had done something to prevent Cormac from reaching this place, had he been able to send me along on his own?

The gates swung closed behind us with a clank and as soon as I heard the sound, the field we were standing in vanished. We were now standing in an open stone paved receiving area. A row of stables was on my right. To my left were several carriages and carts parked in a line. Fae walked back and forth through the space with purpose, not even pausing to gaze at the newcomers. All of them were wearing the burgundy and gold that I'd come to associate with Tiana. Perhaps they weren't her guards in the first place. She must have borrowed guards from the Queen.

In the distance, I saw a towering gray stone castle. We were still a fair distance from it, but we were here. A sobbing sound escaped my mouth as a mixture of relief and fear tumbled through me. I wanted to meet the Queen. I wanted to ask her if Tiana's words were correct. Was the Queen really my mother? It would explain so much. But I was afraid of how she'd react after my experiences with Tiana.

We walked past the stables and the rows of carriages until we reached another gate. This one was connected to a wall that enclosed the castle beyond. At the gate, two guards waited at attention.

"We've got a prisoner for interrogation," the guard holding me said.

"Prisoner?" I realized I'd never explained myself or asked what they were planning to do with me. "No. I'm here to see the Queen."

The guard holding me looked like he was holding back a laugh, but didn't respond to my words. "We'll take her to the holding cell."

"No," I said. "No cell. Take me to the Queen, now."

The guard tugged my arm, pulling me closer to him. "We don't take orders from traitors."

"I'm not a traitor. I don't understand what's happening," I said. "Please, I just need to speak to the Queen."

"I understand you have a prisoner to process?" a new voice asked.

I looked up at the gate to see a guard standing behind the gate. "I'm not a prisoner."

He lifted an eyebrow. "Where did you find this female?"

"She slid right in front of the Palace entrance and then called to a dozen Somalis. I think she meant to attack the Queen," the guard holding me said.

"Open the gate," the new guard said.

"Please," I tried again, "I'm here to see the Queen."

"I know you are," the new guard said. "And you will. Let her go. You all return to your posts. I'll take her from here."

"You want to take the glory from me?" the guard holding me tugged my arm so hard I grunted against the strain.

"Let go of me," I said.

"Let her go, private," the new guard said.

Reluctantly, the private let go of my arm. "Yes, General."

"My lady, I apologize for the reception you received, the Queen is ready to see you now." The General inclined his head.

I heard the gasps and shuffling feet behind me as the guards who had collected me backed away from the General. Not looking back at them, I walked through the gate.

The General offered his elbow to me and I accepted. "Thank you."

"You're welcome, My Lady," he said. "I'm afraid your existence is a secret. Only three of us knew you lived. Less than ten knew you were even born."

My jaw dropped open at his words. "You know who I am?"

"Of course," he said. "I arranged the payments to your father to keep you hidden."

I stopped walking. "You did that? For how long?"

He turned to look at me. "From the day Nani arrived. She didn't exactly look human when she first arrived in the human realm."

My chest tightened. "He knew the whole time? You were paying him the whole time?"

"With bonuses every year on your birthday," the General said.

My throat tightened. I'd never been treated the same as Rose. And he was in a rush to marry me off before her, but I didn't realize he'd known for so long. All this time, the wealth he had, the status he was buying, the business decisions and closed-door meetings had been a lie. "How much money?"

"Enough to keep you happy and cared for," he said.

"Enough to help my father climb the social ladder," I grumbled.

"None of that matters now," he said. "Now, you're here. Everything is about to change for you."

"It already has," I said.

"Come, time for you to meet the Queen."

I took slow breaths in and out and focused on setting one foot in front of the other as I walked alongside this stranger. That was what my life had become. A series of exchanges with strangers. Even the family I'd thought were mine were strangers now. My heart ached for someone who would make me feel like I wasn't so alone. I needed my princes.

I stopped walking again. "I was with the Autumn Prince and the Winter Prince when I was sliding. Something happened. Have you heard any word on them?"

"No," the General said. "But I'll ask for you."

# Chapter Twenty-Seven

❦

Knots twisted in my stomach, my palms were damp, and my heart beat thundered in my ears. We were stopped now in front of a set of large double doors that reminded me that I was about to meet the ruler of Faerie and even if she was blood, I still felt like a nobody.

I glanced down at my muddy dress and took in the dirt in my fingernails. I was sure my hair was nothing but tangles and probably full of enough twigs and leaves to make a bird's nest. I didn't look the part of a lady, let alone Princess.

I wanted to say something to the General standing beside me but I couldn't form my thoughts into coherent speech. He gave a subtle nod to the guard stationed on either side of the doors and they were swung open to reveal a stunning throne room.

Dark polished wood floors spanned the expansive room all the way back to a raised platform on the opposite end. A single, large gold and ruby encrusted throne held a female Fae in a gold dress. Her blonde hair was arranged on top of her head in a perfect spiral of curls and twists that would have made Nani proud. A gold crown rested among her curls, glinting in the light.

I couldn't help but smile a little thinking of all the times Nani had done my hair in a similar way to this. It must've been her way of keeping a little bit of my heritage with me even though I hadn't known about it. My thoughts of my maid, my closest confidant, were bittersweet. I still missed her greatly and I wondered if I'd be able to send someone for her now that I had connections to the Queen. Even though the thought of Nani had brought a smile to my face, the stern expression on the Queen in the throne in front of me had not shifted.

I hadn't realized that I was walking, keeping pace with the General beside me, growing steadily closer to the stranger in front of me. When I was a few steps away from the throne, she stood and descended the stairs on the platform until she was on the same ground as me. She was my height, with the same blue eyes and gold hair. By appearance alone, there was little I could do to deny the strong resemblance. My human mother had resembled me, and so had my human sister. I found out it was possible my magic had worn off on them changing their appearance the longer they lived with me. This time, there was no such possibility.

The Queen seemed to study me, her eyes darting up and down as she walked around me in a slow circle. I tensed under her gaze, balling my hands into fists as discomfort wormed its way through me. I felt like I was already a disappointment. Was that why she had sent me away? I tightened my jaw and tried to remind myself of what Tiana had said. She mentioned that Queens were not allowed to have children. The fact that she had sent me away, was not because I displeased her, it was because she was preventing someone like Tiana from killing me. My chest swelled with gratitude. Despite the disapproving expression on her face, this was someone who had tried to keep me alive. I knew protocol would dictate that I let her speak first, but words tumbled out. "Is it true?"

The Queen stopped in front of me, hands clasped in front of

her. She lifted her chin, giving her an even more confident stature than she had had. "I wish you would not have come."

Those were not the words I expected to hear from her. Hadn't she sent me away from my own protection? Didn't that mean she cared for me? "I don't understand."

Suddenly, her expression shifted again and she looked exhausted. "Queens are forbidden from having children. So I had to send you away or have you killed. That lousy human man who raised you was supposed to keep you hidden away in his home until you came of age."

"I heard him talking," I said. "He was about to marry me off. Told my future husband he'd make even more money if he kept me prisoner." I had thought that whoever was paying my father had only paid for the wedding. Now, I knew he'd been paid my whole life."

"He was supposed to keep you in his home until you turned twenty, then he was free to marry you off. I knew that if you were anything like me, your magic would be triggered by stress. Even in the human realm, where it's harder for magic to show through, someone with all four Courts worth, the magic would have a hard time masking it in situations where they felt at risk. An arranged marriage probably made you quite anxious, am I right?"

I nodded.

"That man was an idiot," she said. "Forcing you into marriage jumpstarted your powers which attracted the beasts that came after you." She shook her head.

"How do you know all this?" I asked, feeling a little hurt. If she had known about the attack on my wedding day, why hadn't she intervened sooner? Why put me through everything I had been through?

"Three days ago, my old handmaid found her way back to me. So I started to search for you. Imagine my surprise when I found out you'd ended up in the Winter Court," she smirked.

My heart leaped. "Nani?"

"Yes," she said.

"She's here?" I asked.

"Yes." She put her hand out, indicating that she wanted me to wait. "Before you say anything more, you will be able to see her, but not right now. Right now, we need to discuss some things."

I nodded, thinking of all the unanswered questions floating in my mind. Though, there was one thing that stood out more than anything else, a single question burning inside me with such intensity that it was painful.

As if she could sense my thoughts, the Queen's brow furrowed. "What is it?"

"My friends," I said. "I don't know where they are."

She turned to the General.

"She was accompanied by both the Winter and Autumn Prince before she fell. They were sliding together," he said.

"And your sister," I added. "I think she's the one at fault for causing my fall. She..."

The Queen's expression darkened. "Hold that thought. We'll discuss your test in private. Not here."

I swallowed, wondering if I should have pressed on more about Tiana's attempt to kill me. Pursing my lips, I lowered my eyes, feeling defeated. I knew there were protocols in royal courts. And I knew there was danger in accusing someone high ranking of any wrong doing, even if they were guilty. I'd been raised to believe that speaking about family was a private conversation regardless of rank.

"The princes?" I asked. "I was traveling with the Spring and Summer princes as well, but they stayed behind to take care of a tear they found to the Under. I'd like to know if they're all safe."

The Queen turned from me, back to her General. "Find out whatever you can on the four princes and report back to me immediately. We'll be in my private chambers."

She turned to me. "This way."

I followed, feeling some of the tension releasing now that I knew the whereabouts of the princes was being looked into. I wanted them to be safe. I needed them to be safe. The longer I stayed apart from them, the more anxious I was feeling. Hopefully, I'd be reunited with them soon.

# Chapter Twenty-Eight

❧❦❧

We took turn after turn down long hallways. Past closed doors, sitting rooms, a music room, and what looked like a ballroom. Finally, we stopped at an unsuspecting closed door at the end of a dark hallway. It seemed like we were in a seldom used part of the castle, away from most of the activity.

"Wait here," the Queen said to the guards who had followed us. Then, she opened the door and stepped inside.

I followed her into a simple sitting room. Rough wood floors were covered in burgundy and gold rugs. Two oversized tan chairs faced a fireplace, a small table in between them.

The Queen settled into one of the chairs and gestured for me to sit in the other. I obliged, a shiver running through me as I recalled a similar meeting with Tiana.

A knock sounded on the door and the Queen and I both turned.

"Come in," she called.

A blue dressed servant stepped into the room, a tray with a teapot, cups, and a few sweets in her hands. She kept her eyes on the ground as she walked into the room. After setting the tray on the small table between us, she curtseyed. "Will that be all, Majesty?"

The Queen waved her hand dismissively. "Yes, that's all."

"Thank you," I called after the servant.

The Queen's brow furrowed, but she didn't comment on my words. Instead, she poured two cups of tea. After adding a cube of sugar to hers, she took it in her hands and leaned back causally against the chair. "This is my private space. Nobody is allowed in here without my permission."

I took the other cup of tea and tried to find a comfortable position. "It's nice."

"If you'd believe it, this is much more similar to what I grew up with. The rest of the castle can sometimes be overwhelming." She took a sip of her tea. "I can't even imagine how you feel right now."

"Overwhelmed is a good way to describe it," I said.

"It's about to get worse," she said.

My shoulders fell. "What do you mean?"

"You already know that the Queen isn't allowed to have children," she said.

"I do. Your sister tried to kill me. Said you lied to her about killing me," I said.

She sighed and shook her head. "I should have seen that coming. I'm sorry I sent her. She will be punished. But right now, you have more concerning things to worry about."

"More concerning than someone who thinks I should be dead?" I asked.

"She won't be the only one coming for you," the Queen said.

"There were others," I admitted. "In the Winter Court. They wanted to know about Queen's Trial. They were insane."

She nodded. "And they will continue to be a threat to you."

"How do I convince them I have no interest in being Queen? I don't want that. I just want to live in peace," I said.

"They'll never let you live in peace," she said. "Not with the power in your veins. Anyone who wins Queen's Trial will put a price on your head as soon as she's in power."

"So what am I supposed to do? Spend the rest of my life running?" I asked.

"Yes, until they kill you. Or..."

"Or what?" I asked, already knowing I'd take that option. I didn't want to be running for the rest of my life, hunted by people who thought I was a threat.

"You win Queen's Trial. You win, you become Queen, you're no longer a threat."

My blood ran cold. "I don't want to be Queen."

"You don't have a choice," she said.

I squeezed the teacup in my hands, feeling the warmth seeping into my palms.

"You'll have to choose escorts to run with you." She took another sip of her tea.

"What do you mean?" I hadn't even decided if I was really able to run. I didn't even know what it entailed.

"Each Queen needs supporters; confidants. At least one male who will eventually rule by your side should you win."

Another knock sounded at the door and the Queen turned. "Enter."

I kept my eyes fixed on the empty fireplace in front of me, processing everything I'd just been told.

"Your Majesty," the General's voice carried through the room and I turned, hoping to hear word on my princes.

Standing in the entryway to the room were Ethan, Dane, Cormac, and Tristan. They were all here. They were all safe.

I dropped the teacup in my hand and was out of my chair before the cup hit the ground. Overjoyed to see them all alive, I ran to the door, my arms spread wide.

Four males crashed into me, surrounding me with warmth as their bodies pressed against mine. Someone kissed the top of my head and someone brushed the loose strands of hair from my face. I couldn't tell whose arms were whose or who was pressing into which part of me. I didn't care. I felt like I could breathe again.

After what felt like several long minutes, we broke the embrace. Cormac touched my face. "Are you safe?"

"I'm safe," I said, looking from him to all the others. "Don't do that to me again. Being away from all of you made me feel like I couldn't breathe."

"Does that mean you've chosen your escorts?" the Queen stood and walked over to where we were standing by the doorway.

All four princes, including Tristan bowed in greeting.

"Does that mean you're running, love?" Dane asked. "Joining Queen's Trial?"

"I don't think I have a choice," I said.

"I'm in if you are," he said.

"You're still under my protection, so I'll go where you need me," Cormac said.

"You know how I feel," Ethan said.

I smiled, feeling like maybe I could handle whatever it was that Queen's Trial was going to throw at me if I had them by my side.

"That's beautiful," Tristan said. "But you're all forgetting one thing."

I turned to look at the handsome Winter Prince, my brow furrowing.

"She owes me a favor, and it's time for me to collect."

# Author Notes

Thank you for taking the time to read my book! I hope you enjoyed your time with Cassia and her princes!

Court of Lies is available for Pre-Order on Amazon

Want updates, news, and giveaways?
Join My Mailing List

**Also by Dyan Chick**
Magic Born, Dragon Mage Book 1
Magic Awakens, Dragon Mage Book 2
Magic Rising, Dragon Mage Book 3
Magic Returns, Dragon Mage Book 4
Fae Cursed: Legacy of Magic Book 1
Dark Fae: Legacy of Magic Book 2
Heir of Illaria: Book 1 of the Illaria Series
Oracle of Illaria: Book 2 of the Illaria Series
Battle of Illaria: Book 3 of the Illaria Series